Vangie
The Ghost of the Pines

Ann Fears Crawford

EAKIN PRESS ◆ Austin, Texas

Cover design by Virginia Gholson Messer

FIRST EDITION
Copyright © 2002
By Ann Fears Crawford
Published in the United States of America
By Eakin Press
A Division of Sunbelt Media, Inc.
P.O. Drawer 90159 ⌂ Austin, Texas 78709-0159
email: sales@eakinpress.com
⌨ website: www.eakinpress.com ⌨
ALL RIGHTS RESERVED.
1   2   3   4   5   6   7   8   9
1-57168-710-6

Library of Congress Cataloging-in-Publication Data
Crawford, Ann Fears.
    Vangie: the ghost of the pines / Ann Fears Crawford.– 1st ed.
      p.   cm.
    Summary: In the summer of 1947, fourteen-year-old Annie
expects a visit to her grandparents' East Texas fishing camp will
be awful, but a handsome neighbor boy and his strange sister
who lives in the woods turn things around.
    ISBN 1-57168-710-6
    [1. Family life–Texas–Fiction. 2. Country life–Texas–Fiction.
3. Interpersonal relations–Fiction. 4. Missing children–Fiction.
5. Coming of age–Fiction. 6. Texas–History–20th century–Fiction.]
I. Title: Vangie, the ghost of the pines. II. Title.
PZ7.C854 Van 2002
[Fic]–dc21   2002152443

For Isabella and Kate,
Margaret and William,
Makayla and Zachary,
and Emmy,
and in loving memory of
John Huey Fears and Alvin Felix Goodhue.

Contents

A note to the reader

As *Vangie: The Ghost of the Pines* is a novel of memory, many of the characters are based on my family. The setting is an actual one, as seen through a young girl's eyes. However, all other characters and events are from the author's imagination and are fictional.

—ANN FEARS CRAWFORD

CHAPTER 1

A Doomed Summer

"This is going to be the worst summer of my life!"

I groaned and pulled the covers over my head. I wished I'd died rather than come down with the chicken pox.

Ozella snatched the covers from me and smoothed the sheets. "God gives us trials and tribulations to make us stronger. Chicken pox is yours."

"Well, God just didn't understand how important Camp Windemere is to me," I wailed.

"God understands everything." Ozella yanked the sheets with a vengeance. "Even whiny, fourteen-year-old girls."

"If God understood me, he wouldn't have given me a fever and a sore throat and had me covered in red, itchy sores. Oh, I could just die!"

I flopped a pillow over my head, praying with all my heart for a quick death. Ozella jerked the pillow off me, thumped it, and placed it behind my head where it belonged.

"God sends us plagues to teach us lessons. Maybe yours is humility. I shore don't see much of that around here."

"God just doesn't understand how much I wanted to go to camp this summer." I was determined to out-argue Ozella. "Instead of lying around in this bed, I could be riding horses in the Hill Country . . . paddling a canoe down the Guadalupe River."

"Guess horses and canoes ain't in God's plan for you this summer."

"God's sure some planner," I grumbled. "Vallie Jean and Sissie will be sitting around the campfire at the sing-along and cheering the Cheyennes on to victory on field day. And here I'll be. Itching myself to death."

"Folks don't usually die of chicken pox." Ozella waved her feather duster at me. "Leastways I know about. 'Course, Miss Annabelle Callista Brooks might just be the first."

"What about my speech?" I wailed. "I've had to miss the whole last week of school and the class picnic. You know I was chosen to give the class speech. I didn't even get to give it."

Ozella would never understand my heartbreak over that speech. With me sick in bed, Mary Martha Austin, that prissy prune, got to give my speech. My speech!

The very words I had slaved over for three whole months had been declaimed by stuck-up Mary Martha. I'd never get over that! Tears rolled down my cheeks.

"Sugar girl, you lie back now and calm yourself. You gonna make yourself sicker, and your pa'll be havin' conniption fits. I'm gonna fix you a nice glass of lemonade. Somethin' sweet for that sour disposition."

Ozella gathered up her duster and cleaning rags and waddled out the door, mumbling about trials and tribulations. Something I sure understood. My eyes were sticky from tears, and I closed them, thinking real hard about death by chicken pox.

I opened my eyes to see Pa, usually my champion and defender, leaning over me.

"How's my girl?" He smiled at me, picking up my wrist and slipping a thermometer into my mouth.

"Dying," I mumbled around the thermometer.

"That bad, huh?" He busied himself reading the thermometer, shaking it down, and placing it in his bag. "Well, the fever's down, and I'm the doctor. I think one more week in bed and you'll be able to get up. No wild games or running around, mind you."

"And no Camp Windemere," I croaked. The awful old chicken pox had even infected my throat.

"'Fraid not, honey. Not this year!" Pa peered over his glasses at me. There was no mistaking my anguish. It seemed to me that a trained medical doctor would recognize suicidal tendencies when he saw them, but Pa kept right on talking, as if my world had not come to an end.

"I called Miss Ireland at Windemere, and she'll hold your place until next year." Pa took my little hand in his, as if hand-holding could cure a broken heart.

"Next year! Next year!" I wailed. "I'll almost be sixteen next year! Besides, Vallie Jean and Sissie are there right now, swimming, playing tennis, doing all the things I want to do."

Pa smoothed the covers I had flung aside in a desperate effort to jump out of bed. "Lie back, honey. Chicken pox doesn't cure itself overnight. Besides, I don't want to risk your getting polio in your weakened condition."

In a whirl of French perfume, my mother, Millicent, appeared in the doorway, brandishing a cigarette and wearing her famous "You've done it again" scowl. "Anna, what's gotten into you? Someone could hear you yellin' three blocks away."

"Now, Millie," Pa said, "Annie's just disappointed that she can't go to camp with her friends. It's hard to be sick in bed when all the other girls are having fun. You can understand that."

Pa smiled at me and gave me a wink. Soothing Millicent's feathers was a full-time job for Pa. Millicent flounced into my pink slipper chair and carefully crossed her legs. "What I understand, John, is a foot-locker filled with shorts, shirts, and bathing suits that she'll never be able to fit into next year."

"Annie can wear them up to the fishing camp with Callie and the boys." Pa, sensing my misery, was playing his usual role as peacemaker.

"Fishing camp, indeed! Anna's clothes will come back in tatters, riddled with ticks and redbugs." Millicent gave a shiver, as if she expected ticks and redbugs to come swarming over the windowsill and straight up her linen skirt.

Pa and Millicent argued back and forth for what seemed to be about an hour, with Millicent doing most of the arguing.

Seems like Pa and Millicent were forever arguing—and mostly over me. It had all started before I was born, when Millicent insisted that I should be named Anna after the movie actress, Anna Nagle, plus Callista after her own dear mother.

Then Pa got the best of her. He bided his time until I was safely born and he had certified that I was indeed a girl, which is what he had wanted in the first place.

While Millicent recovered from what she described as the "terrors of childbirth," Pa had calmly added his own mother's name, Belle, to the Anna on the birth certificate. So, I was stuck with Annabelle Callista Brooks! For life!

But Millicent had the final word—as she usually did. Two years later, before she would agree to even consider having another child, she made Pa sign a paper saying that whether the baby was a boy or girl, he or she would be named Hadley.

Pa signed. Peace reigned. And exactly nine months later, Millicent gave birth to "Mommy's precious baby boy," and I was saddled with an impossible brother.

Always in the way. Always right there when you least wanted to see him.

As soon as Pa and Millicent had tired of arguing and said goodnight to me, in came Hadley.

Now, Hadley never simply entered a room. This time he sort of slid around the doorjamb, dropping cookie crumbs all over the rug and grinning from ear to ear.

"Can't go to camp! Can't go to camp!" he sing-songed, staying just out of the firing line of my pitching arm.

"No, I can't!" I croaked, feeling more miserable than I would ever let on to that little runt. "But I have plans just the same."

"What kind of plans?" Hadley's eyes got as round as saucers. Sensing that I was planning mischief, he sidled up to my bedside. I leaned as close to him as I dared get. There'd be heck to pay if I gave Mommy's precious the chicken pox.

"I'm going to the camp with Callie and you boys." I

gave him my wickedest grin. "And I intend to make your life miserable—just you wait and see."

Hadley ran from the room, and I collapsed into a fit of sobbing. No matter how miserable I made Hadley's life—and I sure could do it if I tried—I was doomed to be more miserable. This summer of 1947 was ruined for sure!

Chapter 2
Packing with Callie

Exactly one week later, Millicent and Pa were off for a long-planned vacation, and I was condemned to two weeks at my grandparents' fishing camp with Hadley and my two cousins, Ben and P.D. The boys loved it all—sandbars, fishing poles, and sunburn. Under other circumstances, I would have had a good time too.

But not when all I could think of was Vallie Jean and Sissie laughing and splashing in the Guadalupe River, and me with nothing but old Village Creek and a bunch of dumb boys.

Actually, the camp was pretty nice. Nothing fancy, but lots of room and time for reading and dreaming. Of course, neither Millicent nor her sister Delilah—my Aunt Dee—ever set foot in the piney woods unless Grandpa Zeke ordered them up to a family fish fry by threatening to cut them off without a cent.

It was my job to help my grandmother, Callie, with the packing, and I was trying mighty hard not to let her see how blue I was.

"Better get a move on, Annie," Callie called from the kitchen. "The boys will be here directly." Callie bustled from stove to table, packing food and supplies in boxes from the Piggly Wiggly and into her wicker picnic basket.

That was something to chase the blues away—our first camp picnic. I could name in my sleep exactly what Callie had packed under the red-and-white-checked tablecloth folded over that basket. Cold ham, potato salad, deviled eggs, a jar of little Del Dixie pickles, slices of cake, and fresh peaches. We'd eat it as soon as we got to the camp, sitting on the banks of Village Creek, with an eye out for our cane poles, just in case a goggle-eyed perch snapped up a minnow.

Just watching Callie bustle around her kitchen while packing for the trip, I began to warm to the idea of the fishing camp. "Don't know what's keepin' Dee and those boys," Callie said, glancing at the kitchen clock. "That girl has never been on time in all her born days."

Her daughters remained a constant exasperation to Callie. How simple country people like Zeke and Callie Hadley could have produced two creatures as exotic as the beautiful Hadley sisters was a mystery to most everyone in our hometown.

Many speculated that Millicent would have a brilliant marriage and move off to a society life up East, and that scatterbrained Dee would surely end up a vaudeville entertainer or a circus queen.

But the Hadley girls had surprised everyone. It was Aunt Dee who had "married money"—warm, funny James H. Hampton, who, town gossips had it, "lived off inherited money" and owned the Hampton House, our town's largest and grandest hotel.

And it was Millicent, of the smoldering eyes and bee-stung lips, who, after whirlwind romances with every young man in the surrounding countryside, ran off to New Orleans and married Pa.

Everyone was shocked, for Pa was fifteen years older than Millie and a man dedicated to three things only—the practice of medicine, hunting, and fishing.

Just as Callie and I hauled the last of the supplies into her Ford, Aunt Dee's station wagon roared into the driveway, spilling out boys, dogs, and suitcases. While Tony, Aunt Dee's Irish setter, raced around Callie's garden, Aunt Dee tried to bring order out of chaos.

"Ben, you and Hadley stop acting like fools," she yelled at my older cousin. "Get those suitcases out of there and into Callie's car. P.D., you stop sucking your thumb this instant. It's going to fall off if you don't stop—and I don't mean maybe."

"Dee, for heaven's sake, can't you corral that dog? He's tearing up my zinnias." Callie stepped out on the screened porch, cramming her straw fishing hat down on her head, while I carried my stack of books to the car.

"What are you plannin' on doin'?" cousin Ben asked. "Settin' up a library?"

"To spend two weeks with you and my brother, I need more than a few books." I fixed Ben with a frown, a pale imitation of Millicent's scowl.

While Aunt Dee rounded up Tony, Callie and the boys put the suitcases into the trunk of the Ford. "P.D., stop runnin' on that sidewalk," she yelled at her youngest grandchild. "You know your failin'." P.D. was well known for collecting bruises, scrapes, and bumps. "Get into this car right now," she told P.D. "Annie, hold that boy on your lap. Let's try to get out of here without P.D. breakin' an elbow."

It was a miracle, but soon everything, including the boys, was inside the Ford. Aunt Dee stuck her head through the back window and handed Ben a stack of comics. "This should keep y'all quiet for a while. Mind Callie now," she warned Ben. "Kiss Mama, sugar," she told P.D. "Be a good little boy."

It was Zeke's opinion that Aunt Dee coddled P.D. and talked to him only in baby talk, which is why P.D. seldom uttered a word. Pa worried that there might be a sounder medical reason.

Aunt Dee waved goodbye, climbed into her station

wagon, and flung her last bit of advice out of the window. "Spank 'em, Mama, if they don't mind." Then she was off with a roar and clatter, hell-bent for the golf course and two glorious weeks of freedom from her children.

"Thank goodness!" Callie grunted. She had little patience with either of her daughters, but infinite patience with her four grandchildren. "Let's get goin'."

She backed the Ford out of the driveway, and we were soon barreling down the highway headed for the woods.

There were two places where Callie felt perfectly at home—sitting peacefully on a creek bank, cane pole in her hands, and behind the wheel of her car.

She kept the Ford gleaming to within an inch of its life and in tip-top running order. Zeke was barred from driving it unless it was a dire emergency, and the only other person allowed behind the wheel was me.

On Sundays Callie would take me out to the old Fletcher Road and allow me to practice my driving. Now and then, under her eagle eye, she allowed me to back the Ford out of the driveway and inch it back into the garage.

"Rubber-tired buggy and a rubber-tired hack. Take me to my baby's shack. Sugar babe, sugar babe. You don't love me now." Callie sang away, her head thrown back and her fingers beating time on the steering wheel.

How anyone could keep her mind on singing—with Ben and Hadley scuffling and giggling in the back seat, arguing over who was going to read "The Green Hornet" first—was beyond me. P.D., thumb securely in his mouth, slept, hot and sticky, clutching his old teddy bear, in my lap.

Callie sang the same song she always sang as we drove along. The scenes were the same, and the boys were certainly the same—silly and foolish, thorns in my side, and destined to be for the whole summer. I sighed a sigh of resignation. Might as well settle back and try to enjoy it. This is what my summer was going to be.

CHAPTER 3
Off to the Woods

The highway was a thin ribbon, running through small East Texas towns, one as dreary as the next. I leaned back and began counting turkey-top pines as they sped past. From time to time, Callie commented on the sights that she had passed a million times.

"Look over there, Annie. That old Methodist church hasn't seen the side of a paintbrush in twenty years. Get a load of that barn. Plumb falling down!"

One thing about Callie's running commentary—it seldom required any answers. I just rocked along, barely noticing the familiar countryside, almost as sleepy as P.D. Ben and Hadley were busy reading the sayings on the Burma Shave signs and giggling.

Just then Callie pulled up beside the gas pump cmblazoned with the Flying Red Horse. "Take P.D. around to the bathroom, Annie. He'll wet his pants for sure if you don't." Callie cut off the engine and gathered up her string bag.

"Can we have an ice cream, Callie?" Ben begged. He and Hadley scampered out of the car and hurried into the general store that served as gas station, supply house, and community gossip center for all of Village Corners.

I took a still sleepy P.D. around to the side of the building where the rustic "Ladies" was located. Close by, four old codgers in overalls, hats on their heads, sat hunched on upturned barrels around a makeshift card table, playing dominoes. They looked up briefly, nodded, and resumed their game. For as many years as I could remember, those same old men had been clanking dominoes around in the sunshine.

Getting P.D.'s sunsuit off and encouraging him to pee in the hot, stuffy restroom took all my energy. "Hurry up, P.D., I've got to go too," I told him.

"Can't," he replied, tugging on the straps of his sunsuit. So much for P.D.'s one word of the day.

I buttoned him back into his sunsuit and sat him on my lap while I tinkled. P.D. was the only four-year-old kid you couldn't let out of your sight for one minute.

When we finally dragged into the general store, Ben and Hadley were arguing over whether they should have black walnut or tutti-frutti ice cream. There was no contest, as far as I was concerned. The black walnut was home-churned by Mr. Simmons's wife. It was pure East Texas delicious.

Callie was deep in conversation with Mr. Simmons. "You boys, get a move on. Only one scoop apiece, mind you," she told the boys, as she continued to choose supplies to replenish her camphouse stock.

"A tin of baking power, Mr. Simmons. Clabber Girl, if you've got it," Callie told the grocer. "And a small can of your ribbon cane syrup. I brought along some pecans to shell, and Zeke will be countin' on pecan pie."

Callie could have bought baking powder in town, but she and Zeke made a point of buying part of their supplies at the general store. Kept them in good with the locals and allowed Callie to catch up on all the gossip.

"Mr. Hadley comin' up later?" Mr. Simmons looked over his glasses as he packed the last of Callie's supplies.

"He'll be along late this afternoon. Soon's he closes down the plant." At last Callie seemed satisfied with her order.

"Well, I'll keep an eye out for him. Now, Miz Hadley, I've got a nice wheel of cheese. Gen-u-wine rat trap! Mighty fine!" Mr. Simmons rocked back with laughter at his attempt to be witty.

"Sounds good!" Callie smiled. "You know, Zeke fancies a piece of cheese now and then. Cut me off a quarter pound, and don't forget a big block of ice—wrapped well, mind."

At last Callie was ready, and she herded Ben and Hadley, ice cream in tow, out to the car. I followed with P.D., who seemed to be in some other world, playing with a licorice whip Mr. Simmons had given him.

"Much obliged, Miz Hadley," Mr. Simmons said, leaning into the window. "Always a pleasure doin' business with you and Mr. Hadley. You goin' to get your minners over to Carruthers's?"

"Yep!" Callie moved the gear shift into first and gave the gas pedal a reassuring pump. "I've got to pick up one of their boys to start the engine and prime the pump for me. Zeke won't be in before dark."

"Well, it'll have to be young Josh." Mr. Simmons leaned further in the car window, settling down for a leisurely chat. "Newt's left the place, and old man Carruthers is fit to be tied. He'd counted on Newt to help out, but now the boy's gone over to Nacogdoches to enroll in college. Plans to be a forest ranger. Help put out fires over to the state forest, I reckon. Spend his days settin' up in one of those fire towers and lookin' all around with field glasses. Why in the world you need a college degree for that, I'll never know."

This was the longest speech I had ever heard Mr. Simmons make. I hid my eagerness for this bit of news by spooning ice cream into P.D., who was happy as a puppy so long as someone was feeding him.

I was glad Newt was gone, for it would be Josh who'd

be coming over to help out. My heart thumped at the thought of seeing Josh again.

Mr. Simmons had finally loaded a block of ice shrouded in newspaper into the car. Callie acted as if she had nothing else to do but chatter away with Mr. Simmons for the rest of the afternoon.

"How's Miz Carruthers?" she asked.

"No change there, sorry to say." Mr. Simmons leaned closer. "Zephyr Carruthers just pines away a bit at a time. Never been the same since what happened to her girl. Turrible tragedy."

I caught his mention of the piney woods tragedy and opened my mouth to question him. But Callie cut off my words.

"Don't I know." Callie shook her head. "Well, we best be moving along. I want to dunk these kids on the sandbar before sundown. Much obliged."

Callie pushed down on the gas pedal, the Ford gave a lurch, and we were off. When we entered the woods, Callie took a sharp right and headed the car down the dirt road furrowed with deep tracks from the lumber trucks.

The woods were deep and cool, and I breathed the sharp smell of the pines. We were on the last leg of our journey, and the fishing camp wouldn't be far.

As we rode along, I had plenty of time to ponder the "turrible tragedy" that the Carrutherses had suffered.

CHAPTER 4

The Mystery of Vangie

The sun filtered softly through the pines, dappling the road with late afternoon shadows. The whirr of insects harmonized with the sounds of jackrabbits and armadillos scurrying through the leaves.

But today I only half heard the woodland sounds that were usually music to my ears. I was consumed with curiosity. Why was it that adults always talked in whispers about things you were wild to know about?

From the time I was P.D.'s age, I had heard about Mr. and Mrs. Carruthers's daughter. But every time I got within earshot, Callie and Zeke just stopped talking.

Now I was bold as brass and dying to know. "Callie," I asked, "what happened to Mrs. Carruthers's daughter? Why do people just whisper about her?"

"Went plumb out of her head," Callie replied tersely.

Suddenly, Callie swerved to avoid a limb in the road. "Drat those lumber trucks. They drop more'n they haul."

I knew Callie was trying to avoid the subject, but I persisted. "What made her go nuts? Was she born a little goofy?"

"Young'n burned up in a fire. Just like in the old-time burnouts. She couldn't get to him. You could hear her cryin' out for him all the way over to Shelby County, they say. Her pa and Newt had to hold her back from runnin' into the flames."

"Is she the ghost woman everybody talks about?" Just then P.D. decided to slide down to the floorboard. I yanked him up by his suitstraps and turned my full attention to Callie.

"Yep. Nowadays, she just wanders in and out of the woods. Wild as a hunted rabbit. Plumb shame too. She was the prettiest thing you ever saw. Snow-white skin, and hair as red as the flames that burned up that poor little boy."

Callie slowed down and made a sharp left. "There's the Carruthers place up ahead. Now, not a word about Vangie. Breaks poor Zephyr Carruthers's heart just to hear her name spoken."

Callie pulled up to the bedraggled fence with its gate hanging by rusted hinges. Every time I saw that old ramshackle house, I was amazed that someone as nice as Josh Carruthers came out of such a place.

It was a sight to behold. Everything—house, porch, and fence—were of pine wood, but nothing had ever been painted. Tar-paper roof and rooms in the back that had just sort of been tacked on. There was even an old smokehouse with a bathtub for scalding hogs.

Roosters scratched out a bare existence in the dirt, while pigs ran wild through a ragtag side garden. The entire yard was a hodgepodge of rusted machine parts, old tires, and the funniest thing I had ever seen—an old potty planted with blue flowers, growing right out of where you put your bottom.

With stern warnings to the boys and me to stay in the car, Callie pulled to a stop, got out, and hailed the solemn-faced man and woman who sat in the porch swing.

"How'd do, Mister Carruthers!"

"Tolerable, Miz Hadley. Hot as can be this time a'year." Mr. Carruthers stirred himself, hitched up his overalls, and moved down the steps slow as ribbon-cane syrup sliding over biscuits.

I kept my eyes on his wife, still sitting in the swing. She never stirred so much as an eyelid. Just stared at us and twisted the apron in her lap.

"How'd do, Zephyr," Callie called, then turned back to the man at the fence.

"Reckon you'll need Josh to help you out for a spell?" Mr. Carruthers's words came out as slow as his footsteps.

"Be much obliged if he could come along to help with the shutters and the pump. I'd also like to buy a few minnows from you—and some fresh eggs, if you can spare 'em," Callie added.

"Hens ain't been layin' too good." Mr. Carruthers stared up at the sky as if he expected eggs to drop like raindrops. "But I reckon Josh can rustle up a few to tide you over."

"Fine! Fine!" Callie gave Mr. Carruthers her broadest smile and nodded toward the woman on the porch. "My best to your good wife." She hurried back to the car, and soon we were off again.

I stole one last glance at the dilapidated house and yard. Millicent and Aunt Dee had some sharp words for the Carruthers place. On one of their command appearances at the camp, orchestrated with great glee by Zeke, Millicent had given Callie "what for" for letting us go up the steps of the house to take one of Callie's lemon meringue pies to the family.

"Mama, I don't want my children hanging around that house. No tellin' what they might pick up—ringworm or whatall. The house is like a pigsty, and that yard just reeks of chicken droppings," Millicent had declared with a shudder.

"It's nothing but a white trash hovel," Aunt Dee had echoed.

"Not everyone can be as high and mighty as you two fine ladies. Just remember your own ma and pa were country folk and proud of it," was Callie's retort. "Poor's poor, but poor don't necessarily mean trashy." Callie had gotten in the last word, but she was careful not to ever let us out at the Carruthers place again.

Callie always saw the best in everyone, even in her own grandchildren, and I knew she felt sorry for the family.

Each spring she bought buckets of dewberries and mayhaws for jelly from them, paying generously. I happened to know that she had packed a dozen eggs from the Piggly Wiggly before we left home. But if you asked her why she bought more, she'd just say, "Farm fresh are better." Subject closed.

My Grandpa Zeke set great store by Mr. Carruthers. He paid the old man a fee each year to look after the place, though if you asked me—and no one ever did— Mr. Carruthers never looked any further than his own run-down front porch.

"There's not a better man with a bird dog," Zeke vowed. "And you can't beat Lige Carruthers when it comes to settin' a trot line."

The two men would sit for hours, talking guns, dogs, and where the fish were biting. Old Sport, Zeke's prize bird dog and constant companion, was hand-chosen by Mr. Carruthers from his own litter. From time to time Callie was known to remark that Old Sport cost more than her kitchen stove.

Suddenly, Callie braked, giving us all a good jolt.

"Here we are. Just like always," she smiled. "Ben, you and Hadley, jump out and hold that gate open. Don't want you nickin' the paint on my fenders."

Callie drove through the gate and down to the camp-house, Ben and Hadley scampering behind the car. "You boys, lock that gate good. Zeke will tan your hides if you leave that gate unlatched."

We unloaded some of the supplies and Callie's picnic basket, leaving the heavier items for Josh.

"Scamper into your suits," Callie ordered, opening the front door and letting air into the stuffy dankness of the camphouse. "You boys, change on the screen porch, and Annie and I'll just change here in the kitchen. Josh'll get the shutters off later." Callie issued orders as she pulled swimsuits and caps out of suitcases.

We shed our city clothes faster than you could say, "creek bottom," and were out of the house in a flash. Callie brought up the rear, shouting as we ran, "Watch where you're steppin'! You know your failin'! Don't a-one of you dare go near that water 'til I get there!"

CHAPTER 5

Jumping Right In

We broke for the water, gleefully ignoring Callie's shouted warnings. Amidst a tangle of cane poles, minnow buckets, and the picnic basket, we raced through the woods. Ticks, garter snakes, and poison ivy were all ignored in our burst for the cool water of Village Creek.

We made our way through a veritable fairyland of East Texas wild. All around us rose those silent sentinels, the cypress, magnolia, hickory, and beech trees that sheltered the Big Thicket.

Our destination was the sun-dappled sandbar where we swam. As Callie came puffing up, Hadley and Ben took wild leaps, yelling like crazy and jumping into the water.

"You kids will be the death of me yet!" Callie held on to an overhanging branch and slid into the creek, while I handed P.D. down to her.

It seemed to me that there had never been anything so wonderful as the clear, lapping waters of that sandbar. I shivered and stretched my legs out in a lazy frog kick. Ben and Hadley splashed water on each other, diving down into the deeper water, sending up geysers that sprinkled us all.

"Stay close to this sandbar or I'll wallop the two of you," Callie called. "Here, baby, Callie's brought you some soap to make bubbles with." She turned her attention to P.D., who busied himself lathering up a bar of Ivory soap, sending out bubbles to captivate minnows that swam up and nipped at their rainbow surfaces. A lazy old goggle-eyed perch swam by, cast a wary eye at us, swished his tail, and headed back to the murky depths of the creek.

Soon Callie called us to lunch, and we scampered up the side of the creek bank and waited for her to spread sandwiches. Food never tasted so good as when eaten out of doors. P.D. let peach juice drool down his chin onto his stomach, and Callie dampened her kerchief in the creek and wiped him clean.

"Now, you kids either rest on the bank or fish a spell. There'll be no more swimming for one hour exactly."

Callie threaded her own sinker, cork, and hook and settled back, waiting for some unsuspecting perch to search out a minnow for dinner. Even the boys fished,

Ben with his head slumped down and an old baseball cap pulled low over his eyes. With his eyes on his comic book, Hadley let his line slip down the creek, while P.D. played with Callie's fishing tackle.

The only sounds were the buzzing of insects, the *plop-plop* of our corks on the water, and an occasional exclamation from Ben as he sighted an elusive fish that swam away from his hook.

An hour slipped lazily away, while I let my mind wander to Vangie, Josh's sister, the mysterious "Ghost of the Pines." Where could she be? What had happened to her? No matter what, I was determined I'd get someone to tell me more about her.

Callie and Ben were the only two who caught any fish, and when the sun began to sink behind the trees, we took one last dip in the chilly water. "Get a move on," Callie called. "Zeke will be coming in soon, and we need to get settled in."

Reluctantly, we gathered up our gear and headed back to the camphouse, P.D. skipping ahead of me, and Ben and Hadley dragging their poles on the ground and planning what they would do tomorrow.

Just as we rounded the corner and the camp came into view, Ben and Hadley sighted Josh taking down the shutters. They streaked for the house and were soon unloading the car, talking to Josh a mile a minute. I hung back, just relishing the sight of him.

He was taller and browner than last summer—a red-headed piney woods god in tattered overalls to my adoring eyes.

"Good to see you, Josh." Callie smiled at him. "Thanks for starting on those shutters. Get those boys to help you prime the pump. I want to get supper on before Zeke gets here. Now, plan on coming over tomorrow and helping Zeke set out the trot lines. Oh, and plan on having supper with us. Fish, if we catch any; meatloaf if we don't."

"Much obliged, ma'am." Josh beamed at Callie and then nodded to me. "How'd do, Annie. Pa says you've had the chicken pox. Sorry to hear that. Hope you're better."

I was tongue-tied with bliss. Josh's smile was enough to complete my day. "Yes, thank you. Much better. I don't even itch anymore."

"Great! We'll get in another swimming lesson, if I have time." Josh turned back to the shutter he was hauling down.

"Thanks, I'd like that." I don't know why I always sounded like a scared little mouse when I was around Josh, but he just seemed to take my breath away.

I scurried for the house to help Callie but managed to sneak a few peeks out the windows at Josh on his ladder.

"Get out of that wet suit and help P.D. with his.

Might as well put him into his pajamas. I don't want him out anymore tonight." Callie busied herself taking out cold fried chicken and getting her butane stove lighted. She always took extra pains around the butane, afraid, as she said, that she would blow us all to "kingdom come."

When P.D. and I were both dressed, Callie assigned more tasks. "Get the table set, Annie, and let P.D. carry the napkins in. He likes to feel he's helping. And don't forget Zeke's syrup pitcher. I'm makin' biscuits."

Just then we heard the *toot-toot* of Zeke's truck horn, and the boys raced to open the gate and ride Zeke's running boards back to the house. Shrieks from the boys and Old Sport's joyous barking mingled with Zeke's booming voice. Wherever Zeke was, there was frantic activity. He was soon helping Josh and the boys with the pump.

"Here's water for the dishes, Miz Callie. I'll be seein' you tomorrow." Josh appeared at the kitchen door, smiling that smile that made my heart turn over twice.

"Thanks a million," Callie answered. "Be here early enough to go fishing with us over to Beech Creek. I know Zeke's goin' to want to drop a cork in over there."

"Night, Annie." Josh gave me one of his special smiles.

"I'm lookin' forward to tomorrow." I had resolved to ask Josh about his sister Vangie and to find out more

29

about the fire that killed her little boy. "The Ghost of the Pines" was what people round these parts called her. Just thinking about her gave me the creeps, and I shuddered. It felt just like a snake slithering down my spine.

Supper was a busy time, with Callie and Zeke making plans for the next day. Zeke had only two days, and he wanted to spend all his time fishing. Much discussion took place over the relative merits of Beech or Village Creek for the next day's fishing. They finally decided to drive over to Beech Creek and set the trot lines out at Village.

I helped Callie with the dishes while Zeke settled the boys to bed. "Just one story tonight, Zeke," Hadley begged, while Ben joined in.

"Okay," Zeke agreed, pleased that the boys wanted to hear the old-time tales. "Just one story about ole Br'er Rabbit and how he outsmarted ole Br'er Fox."

"Rabbit!" P.D. echoed, snuggling deep within Zeke's lap.

Frankly, I would have preferred one of Zeke's ghost stories, which might have given me an opening to ask about Vangie, but what P.D., Zeke's undeclared favorite, wanted, P.D. got. I had heard old Br'er Rabbit about a zillion times, but I soon was caught up in his rollicking adventures.

P.D. was fast asleep long before Br'er Fox was stuck

in Old Tarbaby, and Zeke put him down in the little cot beside Callie. While we were engrossed in Zeke's story-telling, Callie had braided her hair and was ready for bed. Soon we were all settled to Callie's satisfaction, and I was tired out from our long ride. I wanted to think about Vangie some more, but I couldn't keep my eyes open. Tomorrow would be time enough to explore the "Ghost of the Pines."

CHAPTER 6
Fishing for Answers

I woke to the sound of Old Sport's barking. Zeke and Josh were already loading the truck, while Ben and Hadley messed around with fishing tackle on the front porch.

Smells of coffee perking and bacon frying signaled that breakfast was almost ready. P.D. sat on the side of my bed, sucking his thumb and staring at me.

Springing out of bed, I jumped into my shorts and shirt and pulled on my tennies. How could I have slept so long! Josh was already here, and I was determined to talk to him about Vangie.

I gave my hair a lick and a promise, pulling it back with two barrettes. Then I pinched my cheeks hard and applied a little Tangee natural to my lips. I longed for a tube of Chen Yu's Dragon Blood Red, but Millicent had put her foot down on makeup until I was sixteen. Sixteen! By that time, I would be a confirmed old maid.

I knew that Callie, whose idea of making up was a swish of Evening in Paris behind her ears and a dusting of Coty powder over her nose, would never notice my light pink lipstick. But maybe Josh would.

" 'Bout time you got up. I thought you'd sleep all day." Callie handed me the silverware and gave P.D. the napkins. "Short breakfast today. We'll make up for it at lunchtime. Give those beds a lick and a promise. Zeke's rarin' to go."

Callie heaped bacon and biscuits onto platters and called the boys. "Ben, you and Hadley wash your hands. Get Zeke and Josh. Tell 'em breakfast's ready."

Everybody trooped to the breakfast table, and Callie let me pour coffee.

"You're lookin' mighty nice today, Annie," Josh said as I filled his cup. I could feel that special warm feeling he always gave me and knew I was blushing. My heart felt like it would beat right through my shirt.

"Guess my Annie got all caught up on her beauty sleep," Zeke smiled. The boys giggled, and I shot them a look designed to kill.

Callie was busy feeding P.D. a biscuit-and-bacon sandwich as Zeke and Josh settled down to discussing the best place to fish.

"Let's get our trot lines out over here, and then we'll be ready to go," Zeke decided.

Why was everybody in such a hurry? I would be content to sit the rest of the day, stealing glances across the table at Josh. But there was no stopping Zeke when fish were waiting to bite a hook.

Callie and I sped through the dishes and spread up the beds, and then I went looking for Ben. If there was one person who knew everything about the piney woods, it was Ben. He knew where every fishing hole was, all about the old Indian sites, and when the may-haws were just right for picking.

"Ben, have you ever seen Vangie? I mean really *seen* her up close?" If anybody in our family had seen her, it had to be Ben.

"Oh, sure, but only once." Ben went right on untangling fishing line. Why did he have to be so close-mouthed, when I was dying to find out something?

"Where?" I asked.

"Down by the creek. Callie and I were fishing, and I went up to get some more bait."

"I saw her too, sure did," Hadley interrupted, wanting, as always, to be the big show.

"Shut up, Hadley. Can't you see Ben and I are talkin'?" I had no time for smart-alecks this morning.

"Go on, Ben."

"Well, she just stepped out from behind a tree. Scared me to death. I just stood there. Couldn't move or talk."

"What did she say to you?"

"Nothin'. Just stood there lookin' at me like some dead person or somethin'. Made me shiver all over."

"How did you know it was Vangie?" I was busting with curiosity.

"Oh, you'd know her, all right, if you ever saw her. I heard Zeke and Callie talk about her. She's got red hair goin' every whichaway, and the spookiest look in her eyes you've ever seen. She's the 'Ghost of the Pines,' all right. I never want to run into her in the dark, you can bet your bottom dollar."

Just as Ben was warming to his tale, we spied Callie waving a dish towel and shouting to us to get a move on. Soon we were loaded up to go. Was I put out! Zeke let Josh and the boys ride in the truck with him, while Callie, P.D., and I followed in the Ford.

As soon as we arrived at Beech Creek, Zeke was in a lather to go fishing, and Josh and the boys were soon splashing through the sandbar on their way to the hole where Zeke decreed the fish were sure to bite.

Callie baited my hook and sat down beside me, P.D. in her lap. I was so put out I could have cried. There were times—and this was one of them—when I wished Pa hadn't set his heart on my being a girl. Why was I always left behind? When would I ever get to talk to Josh?

I flounced about, dropping my pole in the water and upsetting the minnow bucket. While I scrambled for minnows, Callie rescued my pole. "I don't know what gets into you some days, Annie. All that carryin' on will scare the fish away. Now, why don't you just go fish with the boys?"

I grabbed my pole and headed down the creek toward Josh and the boys. After sliding down the bank, I stepped out of my shoes and onto the sandbar.

"Here she comes to spoil all the fun." Hadley stuck out his tongue at me.

"You're too ornery to have any fun." I stuck out my tongue right back.

"Here-here, you two. There's room for everybody in this creek." Always the peacemaker, Josh put a minnow on my line and moved me beside him.

Well, this was the opportunity I'd been waiting for, but I decided to sort of mosey into the topic. "Josh, I've been meanin' to ask about your sister. Callie says she was the prettiest girl around until her accident."

Josh cast his line out into the creek and squinted into the sun before he answered. "Hard to talk about Vangie," he sighed. "She don't come around much. Just roams the woods—like a wild animal. Plumb breaks Ma's heart, not seein' her an' all."

"Can't your pa find her?"

"Sometimes he can and sometimes he can't. When Vangie wants to be lost, she gets lost. These woods can swallow up a person, you know."

I could tell by the faraway look in Josh's eyes that he

didn't want to talk about Vangie, and my heart ached for him. We fished in silence, but I couldn't keep my mind off his sister. I had to know more about Vangie.

A little later I moseyed over to Zeke, who was cleaning the freshly caught fish.

"Zeke, will you answer a question for me?" I was dying of curiosity.

"Sure, honey, if I know the answer. Your grandpa doesn't know *everything,* you know." Zeke kept right on scraping fish scales.

"I want to know about Josh's sister, the one they call the 'Ghost of the Pines.'"

Zeke kept right on cleaning fish. "Well, it's a long, sad story. And Vangie sure weren't no witch."

"Please, Zeke, it's important." My stomach was doing flip-flops as he poured fish heads and guts into a bucket.

"Well, Vangie was a beautiful girl. Pretty as a picture. Hair as bright as a new penny, and eyes like emeralds." Zeke piled the cleaned fish to his satisfaction and wiped his face with his kerchief.

"Go on." I was all ears.

"Well, from the get-go, she was a wild 'un. Lige and Zephyr had a time with her."

"Whadda ya mean 'wild,' Zeke? Did she run away from home?"

Zeke gave me a look. "That and then some."

"What's 'then some,' Zeke?" I sighed. Why did

grownups always talk in circles? Especially when you wanted to know what they knew.

"Well . . . you know, Annie. Sparkin'. Courtin' with first one fella then another. Nearly drove Lige wild. Fellas comin' round the house all hours of the night, and Vangie slippin' out to meet them." Zeke was cleaning his fishing knife, rubbing it over and over.

"Then what happened, Zeke? Did she run away for good?" At the rate we were going, it'd be the end of summer before I knew all about Vangie.

"Ran off with one of those fellas, I guess, 'cause she ended up with a baby. Don't 'xactly know what happened. Or who the daddy was."

"Oh." So that's why nobody wanted to talk about Vangie. "Don't worry, Zeke," I said, "Pa's told me all about where babies come from." I was proud as could be of my knowledge of what Callie called "the birds and the bees."

Zeke breathed a sigh of relief and warmed to his story. "Well, even with that little fella around, Vangie couldn't settle down. Lige built her a cabin down by the creek, and Zephyr kept a plate of food on top of the stove ready for her. She'd leave the baby with Zephyr sometimes, but mostly she took him with her. In a knapsack like a sack of potatoes. Just wandering. Wild as a March hare."

"Was somethin' wrong with the baby? Somethin' that shamed her?"

"Nope. Fine-lookin' little fella. Hair like a fluffy golden dandelion. Zephyr made clothes for him too. Kept him clean. Nope, nothin' wrong with him. What's wrong was in Vangie's head, I reckon."

"Then how'd she lose him?" I knew there was a fire, but I wanted to hear what Zeke knew.

"Well, the little fella was about P.D.'s age, I reckon. Vangie left him alone. Went down toward the creek looking for mayhaws. Little boy loved to eat 'em with honey.

"Poor little tike got aholt of some matches and managed to strike one or two, and that house of theirs was all wood. Dry as cornhusks. Burst into flames and burned quick. Lige and the boys came runnin'. Vangie too. Her pa and Newt had to hold her back from dashing into the burning cabin."

I moved closer to Zeke, nestled in his arms. "Oh, Zeke, that's the saddest story I ever heard. Makes me want to cry."

"Sad for everybody, but sadder for Zephyr. She's got a bad heart as 'tis, and pining away for her girl and that little boy don't make it any better. But Josh came out a hero. Tried to rescue the boy. Got his hands and arms burned pretty bad."

I knew in my heart of hearts that Josh had done everything possible. He was—and always would be—a hero to me.

"Now, let's get these fish to Callie 'fore she comes out here wavin' that frying pan. Boys and Josh'll be comin' back from storin' the fishing poles and tackle, and wantin' their supper. And Annie, don't be talkin' about Vangie. Some things are best left alone."

Zeke and I walked back to the house, Zeke carrying the fish and I holding his other hand. I cut up potatoes and celery for salad, while the boys, Josh, and Zeke played dominoes until supper was ready.

With the boys cracking jokes, and Zeke and Josh telling fish stories, supper was a noisy affair. But I was thinking about Vangie and just pushed my food around on my plate. From time to time, I stole a glance at Josh. My hero!

After supper, Zeke left for town with the boys hanging on him and P.D. riding on his shoulders out to the truck. When Josh headed out to the pump to get water for Callie to wash dishes, I followed him.

"Sure hope we get another swimming lesson, Josh." Just being alone with him made my heart pound.

"You keep practicin', and I'll be back in a couple of days." He leaned toward me. "You're a swell girl, Annie." And then he kissed me on the cheek.

That night I touched my cheek over and over. I vowed never to wash the place where he'd kissed me, and his words rang in my ears: *Swell girl!*

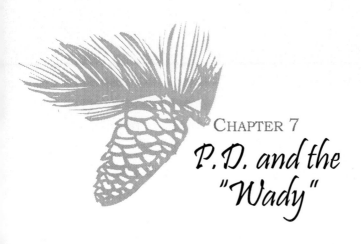

CHAPTER 7

P. D. and the "Wady"

"Ouch! That hurts!" I couldn't help yelling.

Callie was pulling the brush through the tangled nest of my hair.

"Just sit still, Annie! You know Millie wants this hair brushed and twined into curls. *Why,* in the name of all that's holy, I don't know. But she gave strict instructions. Besides which," Callie pursed her lips and studied the effects of her brushing in the mirror, "if I don't give your head a good brushing every day, she'll take one look at you and send you out for another permanent."

Permanents! The mere thought made me groan! Callie knew how much I hated them. But Millicent was determined that my straight, lanky hair be a mass of curls. To me, I looked more like a tousled dog than Shirley Temple!

"That'll do!" Finally Callie put down the brush.

"Keep that hair under a bathing cap when you swim, and we'll pin those curls when you sleep. I don't want to have to brush that mop 'til this weekend. Hear me?"

"Yes'm," I mumbled, dreading the old rubber cap with its strap under my neck. Maybe I'd just choke to death right on a sandbar on Village Creek, and nobody would have to fool with curls again.

"Now, call the boys! I'm gonna make them some Kool-Aid, and you can have a swig of Coke, if you want."

I knew that was Callie's reward to me for sitting through the hair brushing.

"I won! I won!" Hadley shouted with great glee.

"Did not!" Ben answered. "You moved that green marble, sure as shootin'."

No matter what game those boys played, it always ended in an argument. They disgusted me.

"You two, hush up, and get on out here! If you're even thinkin' about Kool-Aid and cookies, that is. Annie, bring P.D.," Callie yelled from the kitchen.

"Come on, P.D." I coaxed him from his circle of toys. "Callie's gonna give you some juice."

"Cookie!" P.D. had heard everything Callie said.

"Yes, cookies too. Come on!" P.D. picked up his old bear and headed barefoot out to the porch, where Callie was serving treats. I was just pouring my Coke when I heard Callie shriek.

"P.D. Hampton! Just look at you, boy! I swear you're gonna be the death of me yet!"

I rushed out to find P.D., standing there, pleased as punch, licking his lips and smiling at Callie. Grape Kool-Aid rimmed his mouth and spilled in sticky streaks down his neck and arms, drenching his sunsuit.

Disgusting! But P.D. just stood there, a silly grin on his face, holding out his cup to Callie.

"More!" was all he said.

"More!" Callie was exasperated. "Annie, take this little scalawag out and dunk him under the pump. Lather him up good with this Ivory, and don't bring him back 'til he's puredee clean. Not one spot of purple juice left. I'm gonna take a mop to this porch."

P.D. screamed like a banshee when the cold water hit him, but I just pumped away. Serve him right if I drowned him, I thought. Still I dutifully stripped off his sunsuit, leaving him naked as a jaybird, dancing around in the water, howling for all he was worth.

"Oh, hush up, P.D.!" I was losing my patience with him. "You used to be my favorite kid, but today you get my vote for pest of the year. You're gettin' worse than Hadley."

I grabbed a towel and scrubbed his little body dry, and soon the sobs became sniffles. "After you take a nap, I'll take you for a walk in the woods. We can pick berries, and you can bring Callie some wildflowers—if there're any left."

"More!" P.D. looked up at me, his eyes big as Moon Pies.

"Well, you're not gonna get any more." I glared at him. Would the crazy critter ever learn? "In fact," I pushed my face up close to his, "there isn't any more. Understand? You spilled it all over the porch. No more!"

My stern look shut him up—for a little while, at least—and I carried him back, so he wouldn't clomp all over the sticker burrs. At the house I pushed his arms and legs into pajamas, and shoved him into his cot.

I was tired of fooling with him and glad when Callie ordered us down for naps. "Watch those curls, Annie!" she warned.

She settled on her bed, patching one of Zeke's old shirts. Ben and Hadley, wearing only their undershorts, were arguing over their comic books, while P.D. snuffled in his sleep, thumb in his mouth, clutching his teddy bear.

I settled down to read my book, *Girl of the Limberlost,* an old favorite I had pulled from my bag. I never tired of reading it. But with the heat, the *creak-creak-creak* of the old ceiling fan overhead, and Callie's humming, I was soon sound asleep.

• • •

"Get those shoes tied, Hadley Brooks, and step on it!" Callie's voice woke me from my nap. I turned over, feeling as sticky as P.D. soaked in Kool-Aid.

"Why do I have to go, Callie? Ben gets to stay here!" Hadley whined, fumbling with his tennis shoes and socks.

"'Cause I need some help with the groceries, that's why." Callie gave her straw hat a thump and picked up her purse. "Ben stays here 'cause he's responsible. He gets to be in charge when I'm not here."

"I'm 'sponsible too!" Hadley knotted the laces and stood up, his face one complete scowl.

"You are many things, Hadley," Callie sighed, "but responsible is not one of them. Now, get a move on. Time and I wait for no one—especially you!"

"All right. Just hold your horses!" Hadley slammed his baseball cap on his head.

"Callie, I promised P.D. we'd go for a walk!" I said.

"Well . . ." Callie pursed her lips. "I guess a short walk won't hurt. But keep a close watch on P.D. You know his failin'. He's just as likely to go off following a squirrel to the end of Creation. And Ben, you go with them. Keep care of things. I'll be back in two shakes of a lamb's tail."

With Hadley dragging in her wake, Callie was off to the Corners and her weekly shopping. I got up and pulled on my own tennies. My head was so fuzzy, I thought a walk might do me some good.

"Up and at 'em, ole buddy," Ben told P.D.

I scrounged around until I found some syrup buckets for our dewberries. Then we were off, Ben in front, me in the middle, with P.D. dragging his teddy bear, bringing up the rear.

Every time Ben spotted a bird's nest or a puff ball he wanted for his collection, we had to stop while he investigated.

"You've got the largest collection of sticker burrs around. Why do you want any more?" I was out of sorts with the world and with Ben too.

"Specimens. Rare specimens of East Texas flora." Ben loved using big words to describe small stuff.

"Sticker burrs and pine needles, if you ask me," I snorted.

"Nobody did." Ben wandered off, poking under logs and peering into woodpecker holes.

P.D. and I picked dewberries off an old fence until our buckets were almost full. P.D. ate as many as he put in his bucket, but I eyed our buckets and knew we had enough for one of Callie's cobblers.

"Let's go find some water and wash up." P.D. followed me into the woods, and we found a little pool of water close by an old oak. It was almost as dirty as we were, but I washed the juice off P.D. and then turned to my own berry-stained hands.

Wiping my hands on my shorts, I turned back to take P.D.'s hand. But where was he? Nowhere to be found. Gone! I was terrified! Lost in those woods with the sun going down.

"P.D.!" I yelled at the top of my lungs. "Hey, P.D., where are you, boy?"

I stumbled through a tangle of vines and tree roots, shouting as I went. "Ben . . . Ben! Come quick! P.D.'s gone."

Then I stopped in my tracks. There he was. Standing as still as a ghost, caught in the last rays of sunlight. His arms outstretched in front of him.

Facing him was the wildest creature I'd ever seen. I knew in a flash that it was Vangie. She was every bit as spooky as people said, but not scary dangerous, mostly just wild and sad looking.

She stood silhouetted against the dying sun, twisted skeins of wild red hair swirling around her pinched face. A tattered print dress hung limp as a dishrag on her body, and on her feet were scuffed tennis shoes missing all their ties. She had the saddest eyes I'd ever seen, pale green and watery like the bottoms of Coke bottles. And they were staring straight at P.D.

Slowly she raised one arm toward P.D. Then, as suddenly as she had appeared, she turned and was gone, melting into the woods, becoming one with the oaks and pines.

"P.D.," I croaked. My breath came in puffs, and I grabbed him to me.

"Wady," he answered, motioning toward where Vangie had stood.

47

Just then Ben came clomping through the underbrush, dragging his specimen sack. "What's up, Annie?
Why all the yellin'?"

"Oh, Ben, Ben." I'd never been so glad to see anyone.
"I saw her. Right there."

"Saw who?" Ben looked around and back at me.

"Vangie . . ." I breathed the name, afraid even to say
it for fear she'd come back.

"Vangie. You mean right here? And I missed her?"
Ben looked all around. "What was she doing?"

"Lookin' . . . just lookin' at P.D. And he was lookin' at
her." I knew my words sounded foolish even as I said
them.

"Wady." P.D. stretched out his hand again and
started toward the woods where Vangie had gone.

I caught hold of his sunsuit strap and pulled him as
close as I could, holding on for dear life.

"She didn't say anything? Didn't do anything?" Ben
looked at me as if I was some kind of fool.

"No. Just raised her arm toward P.D. and then ran
away." I gathered up our buckets and handed P.D. his. I
couldn't wait to get out of there.

"Shoot. I wish I'd gotten another look at her." Ben
took P.D.'s hand and led us out of the woods. My feet
felt like they had rocks tied to them. But all I wanted
was to get home.

We walked in silence, the last of the sun's rays dappling the road. I kept my eyes glued on P.D., walking along in front of me, pretty as you please, just as if nothing had happened.

Ben broke the silence. "Probably thought P.D. looked like her little boy. The one who died in the fire."

"Probably," was all I could murmur. I trembled, still scared to death.

As we got closer to the camphouse, Ben stopped. "Annie." His voice was low and serious. "Let's make a pact. Let's swear right here and now not to tell Callie about seeing Vangie. We'd never get out of the house again, and I want to look for a monarch butterfly as soon as I can."

"Okay," I said. Relief flooded over me. I wasn't as scared of Vangie as I was of Callie knowing I'd let P.D. wander off.

"Scout's honor." Ben looked at me as if I were one of his specimens.

"Scout's honor," I promised.

Then we both looked at P.D., scuffing his shoes in the dirt road. He looked up at both of us and smiled, stretching his arms out toward the woods.

"Wady," he whispered.

Chapter 8

Bear in the Woods

Callie was pleased as punch to get the dewberries, and I was a model grandchild. Helping with supper. Drying dishes without a whimper. Scurrying around the kitchen, putting the supper things away.

All the while, I kept an eye on P.D., but Ben was being a good scout. Keeping P.D. busy and out of Callie's way.

I breathed a sigh of relief. Seems like Ben and I were going to get through the night without a word from P.D. about "wady" or any of our adventures.

When it was time for bed, I got my book and settled down to read. Ben and Hadley were busy with one of Callie's hatpins, pushing it through the screen at a daddy longlegs, and laughing to beat the band.

Suddenly, P.D. jumped down from his cot and began

peering under beds. "Bear, bear," he cried as he searched.

"Hush, baby, we'll find your bear." Callie began rustling through the covers on his cot.

I froze. Ben looked over at me. I shook my head. I hadn't seen that bear since we left the woods.

"Annie, where's P.D.'s bear? I'll never get him to sleep without it." Callie turned an accusing eye on me.

I buried my head in P.D.'s swarm of toys, looking frantically for a bear I knew was not there. "Here, baby," I said in my brightest voice. "Here's ole monk. He needs a good cuddle right next to you." I pulled out a dilapidated stuffed monkey with a bright red smile that had been P.D.'s favorite before bear came along.

"*No-o-o-o!*" P.D. wailed, burying his head in Callie's chest. "Bear!"

I sighed. Once P.D. got something in his mind, there was no changing it. Bear he wanted, and bear he was determined to get.

"Ben, have you seen your little brother's bear?" Callie rocked P.D., making soothing sounds.

"No, ma'am," Ben replied, smooth as butter melting on cornbread. "Haven't seen ole bear at all."

Ben came over to P.D. and took the monkey from me. "But let's see what we have here, P.D. A lonely ole monkey's what I see. How about you?"

Jiggling the monkey close to P.D., he tried to hold

his attention. "Yep, poor ole monkey. Left behind." Ben continued playing with monkey, pushing him closer to P.D. "I just bet old Mr. Ted Bear's gone out in search of some honey pots. Lookin' for honey those bees stored in some ole pine tree. And poor ole monkey got left behind. Monkey's sad and needs a cuddle from Mr. P.D. Hampton. Sure as shootin'."

P.D.'s arm shot out, and he grabbed the monkey. Holding the stuffed animal close, he began sucking his thumb and crooning. I vowed then and there that I'd be my cousin Ben's slave for life. He'd saved the day! And our hides!

Callie lowered P.D. onto his cot, smoothing the sheets around him. "Thank goodness," she whispered. "Now, Ben, as soon as breakfast's over in the morning, you and Hadley go lookin' for that child's bear. Search all the way to Woodville if you have to. But find that bear."

"Yes'm," Ben replied and slunk off to bed. I headed for my own bed and settled down to read. At least P.D. hadn't started crying for "wady."

Night settled quickly over the thicket. The shadows slid down the pines, and dark hunkered in. The only sound was an old hoot owl trilling his night song. Soon everyone was asleep, and I closed my book, thumped my pillow, and joined them.

• • •

Suddenly, I was wide awake. I don't know how long I had slept, but it was still night. And something had waked me. Something—or somebody—stirring in the yard. A wind had come up out of the creek bottoms, rustling the pines. But this was a sound closer to the house.

I just lay there, bathed in sweat. I was tempted to pull the covers over my head and go back to sleep, as soon as I could stop shivering with fear. But my curiosity got the best of me.

Slowly, I sat up in bed, peering over the windowsill. Night held the woods close. A flat, round moon hung high in the sky, its beams bright as floodlights at the East Texas fairgrounds. I could see half of the yard, bright as day, but the other half lay in shadow.

There was no doubt about it. Something—or somebody—was creeping closer to the house. All the haunt stories Zeke had ever told us flashed through my mind. But haunts were for little kids like P.D. Still, the sound made me break out in goosebumps. It felt like creepy crawlies were zooming up and down my spine.

There'd been stories of the creatures of the Thicket making their way up and out of the woods. I could just imagine that moon shining down on the dark stillness of Village Creek. I could picture its rays making silvery snakes on the water, and some big old scaly gator with sleepy eyes slipping and sliding up the banks, heading our way.

Zeke and Lige Carruthers told stories of bears coming out of the woods, but even in my wildest nightmares, I couldn't imagine bears roaming around in July.

There it was again! A sort of slithering, sliding sound. I couldn't help it. I slid down in the bed and pulled the covers up to my neck. I was as scared as I'd ever been. And maybe even more so!

It could be the sweep of a gator's tale. Or maybe a bear paw hitting the side of the porch. Or it might just be a wild hog, snuffling around looking for acorns.

But whatever it was, it was definitely something or—worse to think about—somebody.

Then all was still. No sounds but the rustling of the pine needles high up in the trees. I lay there, bathed in sweat and terror. My skeeter bites itched, but my hands felt paralyzed. I couldn't even move to scratch.

I lay still, staring at the summer moon. Wisps of clouds danced across its surface, forming more and more frightening figures. Hobgoblins dancing in the moonlight. A witch on a boomstick riding like the wind.

Then the clouds deepened, forming another image. A woman's face, the skeins of her long hair, matted and tossed by the wind, snaking around her face and cascading into the moonlight. Her sad eyes seemed to penetrate to my very soul.

I shivered again, listening. The porch creaked and groaned, then shuddered into silence. Dark shadows crouched around the porch. Maybe the critter had come and gone. Back to its hidey hole. Back to the creek bottoms. What had it been? Who would come creeping up in the night? Whoever or whatever—I knew I had to find out.

Quietly as I could, I slipped out of my bed and stepped into my house shoes. By the light of the moon, I could see Callie's sleeping figure under the covers. P.D. sighed and turned over. I froze. All I needed was for him to wake up and start bawling for bears or "wadies."

When he seemed settled, I felt my way along the sleeping porch, following the windowsill. I came to Ben's bed and sat down on the side. I touched him gently on the shoulder.

Startled out of sleep, he sat up. *"Whaaat?"* he croaked.

"Shh!" I cautioned him. "It's me. I need you to come outside with me."

"Where?" Ben wiped the sleep from his eyes and began crawling out from under the covers.

"There's something—or somebody—outside. Close to the house. Don't wake Callie, but just come along."

Ben slipped out of bed and searched in the darkness for his Boy Scout flashlight. We were on our way. With me clinging to the back of Ben's pajama top, we made our way through the house. Then we were in the kitchen and making our way to the front porch.

Ben held the door to keep it from squeaking, and I slipped through. All was quiet, and we moved forward.

Ben crept as softly as a Cherokee, with me sort of stumbling after him.

When we were far enough from the house, Ben turned on the flashlight, keeping its beam close to the ground.

He shone it in every direction. Toward the pump. Nothing! Toward the old tree stump on the opposite side of the yard. Nothing!

Then he swung the light around. There stood the gate—open! Something or somebody had come in. Something or somebody had crept close to the house. But who or what? And where were they now?

Ben crept closer, shining his flashlight in all directions. He closed the gate and checked the latch.

"Whoever it was is long gone. Animals don't open gate latches. So it was somebody." Neither one of us wanted to even think who it might be.

"Let's get back to the house. Then I'll look around in the morning. Maybe I'll find a clue on the path. Don't want to risk waking Callie. Besides, it's too dark to see down by the creek." Ben looked toward the dark woods and the creek beyond, lying deep and remote, holding its secrets.

I could only nod and follow Ben back to the house. He kept his light down, following its beam. Then he shone it up on the porch, and both of us stopped dead in our tracks.

Something was lying on the top step. We must have stepped right over it. Ben crept forward and then motioned for me to follow him.

It was an animal, all right. Lying there right on the step. It wasn't a gator or a wild hog. But it was a bear. P.D.'s stuffed toy, old Mr. Ted Bear himself. And both of us knew that old bear hadn't just walked up onto that porch.

"Take this and put it under P.D.'s covers. Out of sight," Ben warned, "but so he'll find it in the morning. And not one word about this to anybody. I don't want Callie having a conniption fit."

I could only nod in agreement and take the stuffed toy. We crept back through the house, and I tucked Mr. Ted Bear close to a sleeping P.D. Then I jumped into my bed and pulled the covers as close as I could.

Ben didn't have to worry about me. I wasn't about to breathe one word of our moonlight adventure to anyone. Especially not to Callie. But I knew what he was thinking. And he knew what I was thinking.

There was only one word to explain the mysterious disappearance and reappearance of Mr. Ted Bear. And that word was—Vangie.

Chapter 9

Lessons from Josh

"I swan! Here's P.D.'s little bear! I could have sworn I searched through these covers last night. No sign of a bear then." Callie looked straight at me, waiting for an explanation.

P.D. grabbed his bear, clinging to him with all his might, while Callie glanced at Ben.

"Don't look at me, Callie," he said, all innocent. "I didn't hide ole Ted. Not me, this time!"

Of course, he was right. I'd done it. Both of us scurried around throwing our clothes on as quick as we could.

Clutching both bear and monkey in his arms, P.D. trailed after Callie. "Bacon! Bacon!" he yelled, swinging both stuffed toys with glee.

Soon Callie had both bacon and biscuits on the table, and we were busy planning our day. Halfway through our meal, Josh appeared on the front porch.

"Come on in, Josh," Callie called. "Just in time for bacon and biscuits."

"Bacon! Biscuits! Bacon! Biscuits!" P.D. echoed, swinging his toys wildly.

"That'll do, P.D. Settle down now." Callie filled Josh's plate and poured coffee into a tin cup.

"How's your ma?" Callie slid the Carnation milk can toward him.

"Poorly, Miz Callie." Josh took a bite of biscuit, followed by a swig of coffee. "That's why I'm here today. Want to get caught up on any chores you have for me. Pa wants me to take Ma into Woodville to the doctor tomorrow." Josh turned his smile on me. "Oh, and I need to give Annie a swimming lesson. See if she can master the backstroke."

"Aw, she'll never get it! Better give me a lesson." There went Mr. Butt-In-Everytime Hadley. But not even my bratty brother could dim my joy.

I blushed, basking in Josh's attention.

Josh turned to my wretched, wisecracking brother. "Maybe we could work on your frog kick a bit—after Annie's lesson." Josh ruffled Hadley's hair. "You practice on the sandbar, and then I'll throw you in the deep. See if you drown."

"Dishes can wait!" Callie announced. "Get into your suits—shirts over 'em. I don't want you eaten alive by mosquitoes."

Callie led us to the creek, with me hanging behind, walking as close to Josh as I dared. Ben was off on one of his scientific expeditions, exploring around the edges of the creek. We left P.D., close to Callie on the sandbar, happily making soap bubbles, and Hadley kicking to beat the band.

"That's it!" Josh smiled. "Let your elbows lead out of the water." I was kicking alongside him, struggling to keep up as we headed out into the deeper water of Village Creek. The creek, deep and still, wound through the woods, a medley of green, brown, and yellow water, endlessly twisting and turning.

The willows hung low over the water, dripping lacy fronds like green gauze. The creek was cooler and darker here, the shadows of the pines wrapping around us.

Green waterweeds reached out, floating like thistles against my body, while lilypads, like giant green door-mats, floated on the surface. Minnows frisked back and forth in the sunlight, and I could barely spot Callie in her old fishing hat back on the sandbar.

Like he was fixing to gut a fish, Josh flipped me over, supporting my back with one hand. He knew I didn't like to put my feet down in all the yucky stuff on the creek bottom.

"Backstroke's a resting stroke. Good to turn into when you're growing tired." Josh smiled down at me.

Oh, I thought I'd die right there and sink quietly down to the creek bottom.

"Secret is to move your arms and legs at the same time—pull 'em together, and they'll zoom you through the water. Just don't strain. Let your arms and legs do the work." Josh left me floating and began slowly moving into the backstroke.

I concentrated as hard as I could on getting some coordination, sputtering from time to time as my arms fell behind my legs and I sank below the surface.

"Good going!" Josh smiled again. "Now let's swim back toward the sandbar. Don't want you to drown way out here."

We stroked in silence, Josh keeping a wary eye on me. Gradually, I picked up the rhythm and was only a stroke or two behind Josh. He was right. The backstroke was restful.

Looking up into the sunlit sky, watching the tops of the oaks and pines floating by, I couldn't help thinking about our missing bear adventure.

"Josh, P.D. lost his stuffed bear in the woods." I glanced over at him.

"Too bad!" Josh never broke the rhythm of his stroke.

"Then bear came back!" I watched his face closely.

Now I had his attention. Josh swam over to the bank. I followed close behind.

"Came back?" He cocked an eyebrow at me, no doubt thinking I was as looney as Hadley.

"Well, not exactly. He didn't just walk right up the steps and say 'Howdy do!'" Josh seemed to be only half listening. "I think Vangie might have brought him back."

"Vangie! What makes you think that?" Now he was all ears.

"We saw her in the woods. At least, I think it was her. And she saw P.D. He seemed to take a fancy to her. Then somebody—or something—was creeping around the house last night. Scared both Ben and me plumb silly. Then the bear was just lying on the porch this morning." I glanced at him, wondering how he took this tale. "Think Vangie might have brought P.D.'s bear back?"

A frown crossed Josh's face, and he stared across the creek into the woods. "Hard to say. Hard to say what Vangie might do. I know Ma cries for her every night. Says she's afraid she's just lost to her. A lost soul."

Josh picked up a rock and threw it. For a while the only sounds were rocks hitting the water and the splashing of my feet. A lost soul! Those words sent shivers down my spine.

"Well, better be gettin' back. I owe Hadley a little lesson time." Josh pushed off into the middle of the creek, and I had to stroke like everything to keep up with him.

Josh worked with Hadley while I basked in the sun on the sandbar, listening to P.D. babbling as he played.

"Time to get out!" Callie announced. "We'll all have frog fingers if we stay any longer."

After Josh had checked the pump and the motor in the tool shed, he joined us for lunch. Then he rose to go. "Bye, Annie. We'll have another lesson soon."

"Me too!" Hadley crowed. Josh was his idol.

"Much obliged for working on that pump, Josh. Check in with Zeke this weekend."

Callie and I were washing dishes when Josh appeared again at the back door. "Beg pardon, Miz Callie. Wonder if I could hitch a ride home? My truck's got a flat, and Pa's workin' on the spare."

"Why, of course, Josh." Callie dried her hands quickly. "Ben can help Annie with these dishes, and it'll give me a chance to visit with your ma. Cheer her up a bit."

"You always do, Miz Callie." Josh smiled.

"Just three shakes of a lamb's tail, and I'll be with you." Callie was already pulling on her fishing hat.

"Can I go, Callie? I won't be any trouble." Hadley looked from Josh to Callie.

"Oh, I guess so! Save Ben and Annie from lookin' after you. But mind you go to the outhouse. I'm not stoppin' at every crossroads just so you can pee."

I could hardly keep from giggling. Hadley hated the outhouse. Scared to death of the daddy longlegs and spiders. Ben told him they were just waiting to bite off his tallywhacker. I knew Hadley'd just go behind the first pine tree he could find.

"P.D., hit that cot! Not a sound out of you for two hours. Ben, take charge here. I don't care what you all do, but be back in this house by sundown. Annie, don't let P.D. out of your sight. You know his failin'. And I don't want to find any little lost bears when I return." Callie shot both Ben and me a look that said she meant business.

"Yes'm," we replied.

With a toot of the horn, they were off in the old Ford, bumping down the road. After we dried the last dish, Ben settled down to sorting out his specimens while I read and dreamed, glancing over at P.D. from time to time.

He slept a sweaty sleep, thumb in his mouth, both bear and monkey clutched close to his chest.

CHAPTER 10
Lost!

"Pee! Pee!"

I woke, hot and groggy, to find P.D. at my bedside, hopping from one foot to another. He was clutching his underpants with one hand and his bear with the other.

I groaned. Guess I'd dropped off to sleep, and I was as stinky and sweaty as P.D. Now, where was Ben when I needed him?

"Hold your horses!" I cautioned P.D. Then we made a run for the outhouse. I should have known we'd never make it.

"Peed," P.D. called after me. I turned to find him all smiles. Peed was right! It had run down his legs into his tennis shoes.

"Well, Mr. P.D. Hampton, you can just wait, all covered with pee, while I take a turn." Just to make sure he didn't run for the woods, I took him inside with me, leaving the door open. One thing P.D. hated was to be closed in and in the dark.

I sighed. Life with P.D. was never easy. I took him to the pump, stripped off his clothes and tennies, and pumped with glee. When the cold water hit him, P.D. howled, with delight or terror—right then I didn't much care which one.

I dragged P.D., naked as a jaybird, back to the house. There stood Ben, calm as could be, repairing his butterfly nets.

"You heard P.D. yellin'. You could have come to my rescue." I gave him my rendition of Millicent's looks-to-kill.

"P.D. always yells. He's got Mama, Callie, and you runnin' at his beck and call. He don't need me. Besides, I want to get these nets finished, so we can go out to the field."

"What if Callie comes back? Won't she be worried?"

"Naw. She said we could do what we wanted. And I want to try to capture a monarch for my collection. So get a move on!" Ben began gathering up his nets and stuffing his equipment into his knapsack. He took great pride in his "scientific equipment." A big bore, as far as I was concerned.

I soon had P.D. in a fresh sunsuit, sandals, and a sailor hat to keep the sun off. I knew if I brought him back sunburned, Callie'd raise "what for."

"Try to keep yourself clean, at least until we get back." I gave P.D. a scowl.

"Tennies!" he yelped.

"Tennies are all wet. Remember, you peed in them." I was as raring to go as Ben.

Ben threw his knapsack over his shoulder, and we were off, P.D. in front of me, where I could keep an eye on him. He walked along, humming to his bear and scuffing sand as he went.

Soon as we were out of the gate, my spirits rose. The sun filtered through the trees, and the sounds of birds and insects seemed to work their magic on me. There was something about the piney woods that always made me feel at home. Warm and cozy as a caterpillar.

Ben steered us off the path and toward an open field. It was as if we had left the woods far behind. Here in the open air, the sun shone brightly, grasses grew tall, and butterflies hovered over summer flowers.

I loved the woods in early spring, when sweet-smelling magnolias and white dogwoods perfumed the air. Now only a scattering of black-eyed Susans and yellow primroses garlanded the meadow.

"Goin' to see if I can catch a monarch." Ben grabbed his knapsack and net and was off.

"Flybutter! Flybutter!" P.D. shouted with glee, performing a dance in the sunlight. Wild with excitement, he jumped in circles, his hot little hands reaching frantically upward toward the fluttering creatures, yet grabbing nothing but summer air. As if guided by some inner sense of preservation, the butterflies darted and swooped toward the sun, circling just out of the reach of P.D.'s hands.

Suddenly, P.D. lost all interest in his "flybutters," and shot off in the direction of the woods.

"Hold up, P.D.!" I shouted. If Ben thought a monarch was hard to catch, I'd like to see him keep up with P.D. for just one hour.

"Wabbit! Wabbit!" P.D. sang. Sure enough, there was a little cottontail, hopping through the grasses and heading for the woods.

"Wait up, P.D.!" I called. "Come back here right now, or I'll skin you alive!"

"Annie, Annie, come quick! I've found it!" I turned toward the sound of Ben's voice.

Cupping my hands over my mouth, I shouted, "Just a minute! I'm chasin' P.D." But when I turned back, there was no sign of P.D. "P.D.," I yelled, "come back here right this instant! If you don't come back, I'm gonna tell Zeke on you!"

P.D. never wanted to be on Zeke's bad side. Where could he have gone? No sign of footprints. No sign of a cottontail. No sign of bear.

I plunged on, tripping over vines and roots in my

path. "Yoo-hoo! You little rapscallion! Come on back. Monkey's waiting for you at home."

I was frantic and running out of breath. Low-lying branches caught at my hair. Insects stung my bare legs. Sweat poured down my face and neck. No matter, I had to find that kid. And he'd have to answer to me when I caught him.

Suddenly, I heard footsteps, someone running hard. I stopped in my tracks.

"Whoa!" Ben, mopping sweat off his glasses and breathing hard, appeared at my side. "Don't you go off by yourself. Let's look together. Which way did he go?"

"I don't know." Worry and exhaustion were in every word I spoke. "I turned my back for one sec to answer you, and he was off like he'd been shot out of a gun. Chasing a rabbit!"

"Well, jeepers creepers, there's no tellin' where he is by now!" I stole a look at Ben's face. He was as scared as I was.

"What're we gonna do?" I asked, knowing Ben would have a plan.

He thrust the end of his butterfly net into the ground. "You look that way," he said, pointing over my shoulder. "I'll go this way. Shout often, so I know where you are. Say anything that might get that crazy kid to come to you. Then be back here in ten minutes."

"Okay," I replied, relieved to have Ben take charge.

"Let's synchronize our watches." Ben moved into his Dick Tracy role—playing the great detective. I dutifully checked my Mickey Mouse watch.

"Watch where you're goin', so you don't lose your way. I don't want to have to search for both of you. And Annie, keep an eye on the ground. Look for a shoe, old bear, a button—anything that might tell you which way he went." Ben took up his knapsack and headed off. "Let me hear your voice, so I know where you are," he yelled over his shoulder.

"Sure," I called back, starting off through the trees. I kept my eyes close to the ground, shuffling my feet through pine needles and vines, uncovering nothing but rotted leaves and dirt.

"P.D., oh, P.D.!" Ben's voice echoed from far away. "Gimme a yell, ole buddy!"

"Yoo-hoo, P.D." I followed Ben's example. "Come on. Let's go home. I'll read you a story. *Peter Rabbit,* for sure. Maybe even a chapter of *Water Babies.*" I stopped for a moment, hoping to hear P.D.'s answer. Even calling for him seemed to exhaust me, and I felt hot tears rolling down my cheeks. My legs were on fire. Chiggers and redbugs had made a feast out of me.

No answer, but the whirring of birds far up in the pines. I stumbled on, looking behind every tree. Then I checked my watch. I'd been gone eight minutes, and no P.D. in sight.

"Last chance, P.D.! Come on, ole buddy! I'll let you see the butterfly I've found. Hold him all the way home!" Ben's voice sounded closer, and I knew I should go back.

But I couldn't go back without P.D. What would Callie say? What would Zeke do? Already the shadows were growing deeper. Night came fast in the piney woods, and P.D. hated the dark.

What would P.D. do all alone in the woods? Where would he sleep? Would he be cold and afraid? Crying for Callie—and monkey? *Oh, P.D.,* I thought, *where are you? Why don't you come on out so we can go home?*

I brushed the tears from my cheeks and headed back. My feet dragged. My legs and arms itched. I had never felt so sad, so alone, in all my life. How would I ever face Callie? Zeke? Pa? Millicent's scorn? Oh, and Aunt Dee and Uncle James H.—how could I ever face them?

Callie had trusted me with P.D. And now he was lost! And no one else to blame but me! What could I say? What could I do? No one in my whole family would ever speak to me again!

I trudged back toward Ben's butterfly net, every step torture. I dreaded hearing what I knew he would say. Still I looked up expectantly. Ben was there, waiting, hot and tired as I was.

My heart sank when he shook his head. No P.D.

"Couldn't find hide nor hair of him. Not even one clue. No footprints. No bear. Not even one button. He's gone, Annie, and where in tarnation he went, I don't know!"

"What'll we do?" I felt like my whole body had turned to mush. I wished I could sink right down into my tennies. Throw myself down on the ground and cry my eyes out.

"We've got to go back!" Ben looked straight into my eyes.

"No-oo-oo!" I wailed. "Not without P.D. Oh, Ben, I can't."

"Yes, you can, Annie. You have to! Me too!" My cousin put his hand on my shoulder. "Remember, I was in charge. I left you all, searching for my darned ole butterfly."

His words didn't help one bit. I still felt that horrible sinking in my stomach. I couldn't leave P.D. alone in those woods.

"We've got to get help. Get Callie and Josh to come back with us. And we need to move quickly. Night's comin' on. We need to get back and continue the search."

I felt numb all over, but managed to nod my head. Ben pulled the net out of the ground and gathered up his knapsack. He began walking as fast as he could, and I struggled to keep up.

Once we were back in the field, Ben stopped just as

suddenly as he'd started. He put down his net and opened his knapsack. Reaching in, he pulled out one of Callie's Mason jars, holes punched in the top.

Frantically beating its wings against the jar was the most beautiful butterfly I had ever seen. The wonder of it took my breath away. Its gold-and-black wings never stopped moving as it plunged from side to side, trying to escape.

I watched in amazement as Ben slowly unscrewed the top. With one great burst of energy, the butterfly fluttered free, soaring out over the meadow, heading for a distant patch of wildflowers.

"Oh, Ben," I whispered. "You'd wanted that butterfly for so long. Why did you let it go?"

Ben, his eyes still fixed on the sky where his butterfly had disappeared, mumbled, "I found it. I caught it. Now it's better off free."

Tired and sweaty, dreading what waited for us, we trudged back toward the camphouse, neither of us saying a word.

CHAPTER 11
Desperate Rescuers

I'd never felt so down. Scared too! My tennies felt like they were filled with lead. And my heart too.

"Uh-oh!" Ben pointed toward the camphouse. "She's back, and she's lookin' for us."

Just as I feared, Callie stood on the porch, one hand shading her eyes, peering down the path. It was three of us she was lookin' for, and I hated to think what she'd do when she found there were only two.

"Where's P.D.? What've you two done with that boy?" Like greased lightning, Callie was off the porch, her eyes searching Ben's eyes.

"He wandered off, Callie." Ben mopped the sweat from his brow. "Couldn't find him. We looked everywhere. I thought we'd better come back and get you and Josh. Then maybe we could find him before sundown."

Callie's face was white as a sheet. "What do you

mean, you couldn't find him? You left that little child all alone down by the creek? For garden's seed, Ben Hampton, what's got into you? And you, Annie?"

Callie turned her gaze on me, and I shrank down, afraid to answer.

"Wasn't Annie, Callie. I was in charge." Ben sprang to my defense. "And it wasn't by the creek. It was out in that big meadow where all the flowers are. I was lookin' for butterflies."

"Well, I shore hope you found some, 'cause you've lost your little brother!" Callie glared at Ben. She was back to her old self again, and I breathed a sigh of relief. Callie mad was easier to deal with than Callie scared.

Ben put down his knapsack. It was time to take charge, and he knew it. "Callie, you'd better go get Josh. And maybe send Mr. Carruthers to phone for Zeke. We want to find P.D. before dark."

"Yes, yes, you're right, Ben." Callie slammed her straw hat on her head. "You and Annie go inside. Wash your faces, and get some lemonade or a Coca-Cola. Sandwich if you want it. Don't wake up Hadley. Then head back for that field. I don't intend for that little boy to be lost in the dark for one minute. Understand me?"

"Yes'm," Ben mumbled, and I shook my head. There was no misunderstanding Callie. We were to find P.D.— or else. Ben and I watched the Ford shoot out of the gate, and then we went inside.

75

While Ben gulped down lemonade, I drank a Coke. Neither of us wanted food, but I dabbed calamine lotion on my legs where the mosquitoes and chiggers had attacked.

"How do you think we can find him?" I watched Ben's face carefully for some sign of a plan. "Where haven't we looked?"

"I don't know." Ben was busy reorganizing his knapsack, filling his canteen with water. "Hand me some crackers and some of that rat-trap cheese, Annie. No tellin' when we'll get back."

"You think we'll find him soon, Ben?" The mere thought of the piney woods after dark sent shivers down my spine.

"Stop askin' questions." Ben was clearly out of patience. "Let's get goin'. Maybe P.D.'s just waitin' for us to come rescue him."

All the way to the field, Ben looked to each side of the road as if expecting P.D. to pop out of the pines like a jack-in-the-box. I looked too, hoping against hope that he would. Fat chance! Still I would have given my entire set of Nancy Drew books just for one glimpse of P.D.'s silly grin.

Shadows were already deepening when we turned into the meadow. Ben put down his knapsack near a clump of black-eyed Susans. "Circle over toward the right, but don't go into the woods," he told me. Ben had obviously come up with a plan. "Holler as loud as you can. Let P.D. know we're not mad, just lookin' for him. We don't want him scared to come out.

"I'm gonna do the same on the left side. Maybe we'll meet in the center, but when you hear Callie's car, head for this bunch of flowers and my knapsack."

I nodded, letting him know that I was only too glad to follow his directions. Then I headed through the grasses, calling as I went.

"Yoo-hoo! P.D., it's Annie. Time to go home. Time for supper. Callie's fryin' chicken." I crossed my fingers, vowing to fry P.D. a whole chicken if he'd only show up.

I heard Ben's voice from the opposite side of the meadow. "Allee, allee, oxen free! All come in free!" I smiled at the old saying from a game of hide-and-seek that P.D. loved to play.

Still I trudged on, covering the same old ground, looking toward the woods for any sign of a little boy and his bear. My voice was hoarse; my legs felt like they were on fire. Still no P.D.

Then the *oogha-oogha* of Callie's horn sounded from the road. I turned and headed toward the sound, hoping to see Ben holding P.D.'s hand. But when I got there, I saw Ben shaking his head, while Josh pulled ropes and flashlights from the car.

"Pa's gone in to call Mr. Zeke. He's gonna wait for him and then they'll meet us." Josh handed Ben a flashlight and a coil of rope. "Ben, you and Miz Callie head into the woods on the far side. Annie and I'll explore over there. Use the flashlights if you need them, and look under logs. P.D. might be caught and not able to call out. Use your rope if you have to pull him out."

Ben coiled the rope around his arm, while Callie and I took the flashlights. "Let's meet back here in forty-five minutes, and just hope we find him before then. These flashlights won't be much help when dark settles in." Josh pulled his coil of rope around his arm, and we were off.

Ordinarily, I would have been thrilled at the chance of time alone with Josh in the woods. But now I was too tired and too scared to even think. I just loped along, trying to keep up with Josh's pace.

"Keep your eyes on the ground, Annie. P.D. could have tripped over a log, fallen, and can't get up. Look under every log, every limb. And don't let me out of your sight."

"Think we'll find him, Josh?" My eyes were pleading with him for the right answer. But I got none.

"Don't rightly know. The woods have a way of claiming their own—and keeping their secrets." Josh started off, kicking leaves with his feet, throwing his rope ahead of him.

On and on we went, making tracks through the woods. He called out, "Hey, P.D., ole buddy. It's Josh, come to get you! Holler if you can hear me!"

The only sound that greeted us was the *rat-a-tat-tat* of a woodpecker, beating out a rhythm on a loblolly pine. A solemn-eyed owl hooted from its perch in an old oak. Then, skittish as an old hen, it spread its wings and soared toward the sky.

From time to time a wild-eyed deer skittered through the trees, casting wary glances at us, and then bounded on. Bees buzzed from their hive in the hollow of an old cypress log.

The woods grew darker and deeper, the tangled branches of live oaks shutting out the last of the sunlight. My once lovely, sheltering trees, like giant goblins, loomed over me, dark and scary. Even the smells grew stronger. I wrinkled my nose at the rank odor of rotting plants and decaying leaves.

Night was coming on, and tree limbs seemed to snake out, ready to grab me and hold tight. The moss hanging from the branches swept over my hair like cobwebs, threatening to entangle and hold me there.

I straggled along, trying desperately to keep up with Josh's long stride and falling more and more behind. My legs ached from walking, and I was so hot and tired, I wanted to die.

Suddenly, I burst into tears and plopped down on a tree stump, too exhausted to take one more step. Josh heard my bawling and turned back, stooping down in front of me, his face close to mine.

"What's wrong, Annie? Too tired to go on?"

I nodded, and Josh took my hand in his and drew me toward him. Any other time, I would have been in heaven, but now I was simply too tired and achey to care.

"Oh, Josh," I wailed, burying my face in his shirt. "I lost P.D. Ben takes the blame, but it was me. I didn't watch him close enough. I let him wander off. And now he's lost."

"Hush now, Annie." Josh rubbed my back with his hand. "Wasn't your fault, at all. P.D. goes his own way. Just as likely to wander off with Miz Callie or me. There's no controllin' the boy."

"I know," I sighed, "but it was me he was with. Callie blames me, Zeke blames me, and Pa will blame me too when he hears."

Josh drew a large bandana handkerchief out of his pocket and began wiping my cheeks. The bandana smelled like grease and sweat, but I didn't mind. It was his. My tears dried up despite my misery.

"I don't think anyone's gonna blame you. Least of all your pa. He understands people better'n anybody I know, and he shore understands P.D. I know he worries about his not talkin'."

I knew Josh was running on and on, trying to make me forget my unhappiness, and I loved being close to him and listening to him talk. "Zeke says P.D.'ll talk when he has somethin' to say." I buried my last sniffle in Josh's bandana and handed it back to him.

He smiled as he folded it, tucking it into his shirt pocket. "That remains to be seen. We'll just ask the little fellow when we find him."

"You think we'll find him?" I got up from the stump and straightened my clothes.

"Not if we sit here all day natterin' to beat the band. Come on. Let's make our way back to see how Miz Callie and Ben are farin'. Maybe P.D.'ll be sittin' right there with them, waitin' for us."

But when we arrived back at the meadow, Ben and Callie were alone. No P.D.! Ben looked as frustrated as I felt, and sweat was running down Callie's face.

Josh took one look at her and herded us toward the car. "No sense goin' any further tonight. Dark's comin' in fast, and we've covered as much as we can. Best we wait for Pa and Mr. Zeke. Then we can search again."

Callie nodded and handed Josh the car keys. I climbed in beside him, with Callie and Ben in the back seat. Callie was lookin' out of the window, tryin' to hold back tears, and Ben was strangely silent all the way home.

Once Josh had parked the Ford, Callie rushed inside to check on Hadley, while Ben stored the flashlights and rope. Josh started toward the house to help out, but I caught his hand.

"Josh," I whispered, anxious that Ben would not hear what I needed to say.

Josh turned back to me. "What's the matter, Annie? Still feeling bad?"

"No." I had been thinking all the way home about P.D.—and Vangie. I had to tell someone what I had been thinking about since we left the meadow, and Josh was the one to tell. Callie would "pooh-pooh" my fears, and Ben never listened to me.

"I was just thinkin', Josh." He looked at me with a puzzled grin. "I wonder if Vangie might have taken P.D.? Might have wandered off with him into the woods?"

Josh stopped in his tracks, his grin turning serious. "What makes you think that, Annie? Did you see Vangie anywhere near P.D.? Hidin' behind a tree watchin' him or somethin'?"

"No, nothin' like that," I had to admit, "but you know what I told you about Vangie and P.D. when he first saw her. She lookin' at him, and him callin' her 'wady.' I just thought he might have seen her and wandered off with her. You know P.D., he loves attention, and he seemed to cotton to Vangie."

I felt like a fool. It sounded like I thought Josh's sister had kidnapped P.D. Stolen him from under our very eyes. But Josh sat down on the top step and looked at me, his face as serious as I'd ever seen it.

"Annie, you might be on to somethin'. You did the right thing in tellin' me. Vangie never got over her little boy's dyin' so tragic like. Maybe she thought P.D. was him come back again. What does Ben think?"

"I haven't told him, Josh. Nor Callie. I didn't want to put ideas into their heads."

"Right, Annie." Josh smiled that crooked grin that made my heart turn over. "You're startin' to figure things out like a grownup."

Josh rose and took my hand. "Let's keep this just between us, but I guarantee you, I'm goin' to tell Pa about this. Maybe he can coax Vangie out to talk to us. And maybe she'll give us a clue as to where to find P.D."

Still holding my hand, Josh led me into the house. I felt better about telling him my fears. But I sensed that the worst was yet to come and that finding P.D. was not going to be as easy as we all wanted it to be.

CHAPTER 12
Searching and Searching

I spotted them first. Josh's pa, two other men, and a flurry of bird dogs, bounding about and straining at their leashes. Zeke was there too, with Old Sport, as feisty as the others, barking wildly, and raring to go.

"Sorry about your boy, Miz Callie. But we're gonna find him." Mr. Carruthers tipped his hat to us. "I took the liberty of callin' Sheriff Washburne, and this here's his deputy, Luke Gormsby."

The two men doffed their hats, and the sheriff, without cracking a smile, nodded to Callie. "How'd do, ma'am."

"'Preciate you helpin' find our boy," Callie replied.

"We needed all the help we can get, Callie," Zeke added. "Hard to spot the boy in the dark. We're gonna fan out through the woods with the dogs. Sure to find him soon."

"Yes, Zeke, I'm sure you will." Callie patted his arm and sighed. The presence of Zeke and the other men seemed to lift her spirits.

"Josh, you come with us. Callie, put on the coffee pot and rustle up some sandwiches, if you will. These men will be hungry when we return—with P.D." Zeke turned back toward the men.

"I want to go, Zeke." Ben's voice and eyes pleaded to be included. "I was in charge. I'm responsible for P.D. gettin' lost."

Zeke looked Ben squarely in the eyes. "Nobody's at fault. P.D.'s lost. That's it, and I know you want to help. But I need you right here, takin' care of Callie and your cousins. I need a responsible man if P.D. wanders back. One who'll help Callie if he's hurt, and someone to find us and let us know."

Zeke patted Ben's arm, and Ben nodded, seeming to grow taller with Zeke's words.

"Oh, and Ben," Zeke continued, "I called your ma and pa. Had to have them send someone out to the golf course for your ma, but your pa's pretty broken up. I'll need you to calm him down and fill him in on what we're doin' to find your brother. But keep him here. Don't let him go wanderin' off lookin' for us. I don't need another search party to find James H."

"Yes, Zeke, you can count on me." Ben was all seriousness and importance.

"I know I can, boy!" Zeke ruffled Ben's hair. "Callie, I sent a wire to Doc and Millie out in the wilds where they're fishin'. Whichever way this turns out, we're gonna need Doc. He knows how to handle P.D. No matter what condition he's in."

Oh, lordy. My heart sank. Bad enough for Aunt Dee and Uncle James H. to witness my humiliation, but now Pa and Millie would be coming too. Millie'd be sure to heap blame all over me.

Zeke must have sensed my misery, for he turned to me, drawing me close. "And, you, Annie. I need you to help Callie with sandwiches. And when your Aunt Dee gets here, she's gonna feel mighty lonely without her little boy. You know, she sets great store by you, so I need you to stand by her."

I nodded, a big lump filling my throat. I caught a glimpse of Josh smiling at me and ran toward him. His arm went around me, just as tears started running down my cheeks.

"Hush that, Annie," he murmured into my hair. "Cryin's not gonna help. And it'll just make Miz Callie feel worse."

"But I want to go! I want to help find P.D. I lost him."

"You heard your grandpa, Annie. You're needed here."

Josh turned my face up and looked directly into my eyes. "Tell you what. If we haven't found P.D. by daylight, I'll sneak back here and take you out with me to search. But, until then, stay by Miz Callie and the boys."

With dogs baying at their heels, the men headed for the woods. Callie, Ben, and I just stood there, looking after them, forlorn and lonely without Zeke's presence. Gradually, the shouts of the men and the barking of the dogs grew fainter and fainter.

"All right, let's get inside. Annie, you can help me, and Ben, you corral Hadley. I'm gonna throw together some soup while you make sandwiches, Annie. Those men will be good and hungry when they get back."

Callie swept into the camphouse, with the two of us tagging along. As always, when she was upset, Callie became a whirlwind of activity. Ben and Hadley had to set the table for twelve. I had to make a zillion sandwiches.

"Don't bother cuttin' off the crusts," she said. "These men won't mind a few edges on those sandwiches. And make 'em thick, mind. No need to scrimp."

I sat on the kitchen stool, cutting meat and bread, spreading mustard, heaping on lettuce, slicing tomatoes. My mind was no more on sandwiches than on heaven. I was with Josh and the others, searching the creek bottoms, combing the meadows, looking for a little lost boy.

Oh, P.D., I thought, *if I ever get you back, I'll smother you with hugs and kisses and never let you out of my sight.*

"Chicken legs will have to do. All that's in the ice-box." Callie was busy, cutting up onions and potatoes, slicing carrots, and tossing them all into a big pot. Soon the delicious smell of simmering soup filled the kitchen.

"What's for dinner, Callie? I'm hungry!" Hadley stood in the kitchen door, his smiling face reminding us that life went on, no matter how sad we were.

"Goodness gracious, Hadley Brooks. You'd want to eat if you were in the middle of a shipwreck and fixin' to drown." But Hadley's pleas reminded Callie that we all needed food.

"Soup's not done, but we'll open a can of pork and beans. Set some of those sandwiches out for us, Annie."

"Goody!" Hadley was happy as a clam. His idea of dinner was always something out of a can. Ozella swore he'd die of lead poisoning by the time he was twenty.

Just as we were finishing our scratch supper, we heard a car horn tooting at the gate. "Run out and open the gate for your ma and pa, Ben."

In just a minute or two, Aunt Dee flew right into Callie's arms. "Oh, Mama, Mama, have they found my little boy?" Aunt Dee cried. Uncle James H. stood beside Ben, just looking on, his face a mask of misery. In all my life, I'd never seen anything like the change in Uncle James H. Always laughing, my uncle seemed to have aged twenty years overnight. Now his face was taut and drawn, his hands quivering.

Ben went over and put his hand on his father's arm. "Zeke's gone with the other men, Pop. Said for you to wait here for word."

"Think I ought to join them, Son. Maybe we could go together?" Uncle James H.'s eyes were pleading for some answer, some way he could help.

"Don't think so, Pop." Ben's voice was quiet. "Zeke wants us here in case P.D. wanders back. We don't know how he'll be. You'll have to stay with him, while I go for Zeke."

"Guess that's right." Uncle James H. nodded his head, his eyes vacant.

"Soup's ready! How about a bowl, Dee? You need to keep up your strength! James H., come on in and have a bite." Callie was drawing her family together, determined to make everyone feel better.

I took Uncle James H.'s hand and led him to the table, sitting close by him and Aunt Dee. Callie served soup and kept chatting in soothing terms, but I had never seen her so dejected. And I was downhearted too.

After supper, Aunt Dee went into the kitchen with Callie, and I rose to help clear the dishes.

"You and Ben go out on the porch with your uncle, Annie. I can handle Dee, but he's takin' this pretty hard. Try to cheer him up. Let him know Zeke and the men are doing all they can to find P.D." Callie pushed Ben and me toward the porch, where Uncle James H. was sitting, his head buried in his hands.

Just then we heard the men returning, and all of us ran to the porch. I strained to catch any sign of a small boy with them, but there was none.

Zeke, as downcast as I've ever seen him, put his hand on Uncle James H.'s shoulder. "No sign of the boy, James H. It's just too dark, even for the dogs to catch a sign. We're goin' back with the dawn, and you can come with us if you want."

Uncle James H. nodded his head but said not a word. The look of torment in his eyes was enough to break my heart.

While Callie and Aunt Dee fed the men, Ben sat next to his father, fiddling with his butterfly nets. I sat on the other side, trying to think of something to say to comfort my uncle, to bring the laughter back to his eyes.

Instead, I had to watch in horror as tears slowly slipped down his face. I had never seen a man cry before, and I couldn't bear it. I fled, rushing out into the yard and down to the pump.

But memories followed me like puppies yapping at my heels. Here is where I'd sprayed P.D. when he was covered with Kool-Aid. Seemed like I could still hear his yelps and screams!

Everywhere I looked, there was P.D. Scampering up

the stairs, dragging his bear with him. Clamoring to be allowed to carry the berry buckets. Sitting on Callie's lap and eating cookies, dropping crumbs all over himself.

The thought of my little cousin all alone in the woods made my heart break, and just like Uncle James H., I felt tears, hot as the summer sun, creep down my cheeks. How frightened P.D. would be! He was scared of the dark. Hated being closed in. Never wanted to be by himself for even one moment.

Now he was all alone, scared and hungry, surrounded by the dark, with nobody but Mr. Ted Bear for company. No one to hold him on her lap like Callie did. No one to tease him like Ben did. No one to tell him a bedtime story like Zeke did. No one to dress him and boss him like I did.

Where would he sleep? What would he eat? Would Vangie find him and spirit him away from us forever? I couldn't even bear to think of the creatures and critters out there, waiting to harm a little boy. All I could think of were Josh's words: "The woods have a way of claiming their own."

Would the woods claim P.D.? Did Vangie think he was her little boy come back to her? Would he be one of the secrets the piney woods would keep forever? I shivered at the thought.

Oh, God, I prayed, *let the men find him. Send him back to us. I promise I'll be good the rest of my life. I'll*

*pick up my clothes. Get permanents without squirming.
Even let Millie boss me around without complaining. Just
let him be safe. Send him back!*

Suddenly, they were there, blinking in the darkness.
Tiny fireflies everywhere, swarming out of the dark, circling around me. Embracing me with their tiny, twinkling lights. How many times Ben, Hadley, and I had
chased them and caught them, imprisoning them in
jars just to watch those tiny lights, flickering on and off
in the darkness.

Ben wanted to know what made them work. I wondered where they came from. Where did they go with
the dawn? Now they were here, fluttering about me, lift-
ing my spirits with their fairy lights. Where had they
been?

I hoped against hope that perhaps these sparkling
creatures had circled and swarmed around P.D., making him laugh, keeping him company, their tiny bea-
cons of light signaling his way home.

Danger!

"Annie! Annie!"

I woke with a start. Josh stood right outside the window, scratching on the screen to wake me. At first I couldn't make out what he wanted. I had forgotten all about P.D. and had been dreaming that I was at Camp Windemere. Then it all rushed back like a nightmare.

"Come quick, if you're comin'," Josh whispered.

I was up and into my shorts and shirt in a flash, carrying my tennies with me. Zeke and Uncle James H.'s beds were empty, and Ben was gone too, his covers tossed back. I knew the search had begun with first light.

"Are we going back to the meadow?" I asked Josh. I tugged on my tennies and smoothed my hair. No time to worry about curls today.

"No," Josh replied. "The sheriff and his deputy

combed that area yesterday. I want you to show me exactly where it was that you and P.D. saw Vangie. Perhaps we can find her, and just maybe she's seen P.D."

"Down by the creek and over this way." I took Josh's hand and started through the pine thicket.

Bathed in a soft, dewy light, the woods seemed still and quiet. I had never been up so early, and I marveled at the pink and gold of the sun peeping through the pines. The only sound that broke the stillness was the warbling of some distant bird greeting the morning.

How could a world so peaceful and still at dawn be so threatening at night? How could the tall oaks that stood like guardians of the forest have seemed like terrifying spooks in the darkness?

Once again the piney woods formed a world of serenity, and I felt deep inside that P.D. was safe, just waiting for us to find him. But where could he be? Could Vangie have hidden him?

"This is sorta where we saw her." I motioned toward the creek and Josh looked around, searching behind every tree. No sign of Vangie; no sign of P.D.

Josh bent toward the ground. "Somebody's been here. Leaves are all disturbed, but it could have been anybody. Maybe even the sheriff and his men this morning. Can't tell for sure.

"Keep searching in this area. Look behind each of the trees. See if you see any sign of P.D. I'm gonna

94

search down by the creek." Josh was anxious to cover as much ground as possible. "Meet me back here in twenty minutes."

Then he was gone, loping through the woods like one of his pa's bird dogs. Too late, I realized I had left my watch on the windowsill. But I had to search. I'd just have to think through twenty minutes.

I was determined. Not a log or a limb would be left unturned. Something inside told me that P.D. couldn't be far away. If Vangie had him, surely she wouldn't hurt him.

Armed with a stick, I went through the mass of pine straw and leaves on the ground, picking my way through the underbrush. Squirrels chittered, and birds fluttered in the trees, and I dared not think of what other critters might be hiding in the wild around me. I searched behind every tree, every bush, looking for anything that might lead us to P.D.

Further and further I went, growing more and more frustrated. The woods grew darker and deeper. In the distance I could hear the baying of the dogs and the men stomping through the woods, one of whom I hoped was Josh.

Then I stopped. Someone or something seemed to be watching me. The woods seemed alive with eyes. Could squirrels be staring at me from their nests in the leaves? Was the old owl who hooted in the night keeping an eye on me? Were tiny wild birds spying from the branches in the treetops?

Or was someone lurking behind the trees? Keeping shifty, watchful eyes on me as I moved through the woods? The thought made shivers creep down my spine, and I hurried on.

Suddenly, the natural world around me began to change. I stopped to listen. The chorus of tree frogs grew louder. There was a flurry of animals, a sense of panic to the creatures of the woods.

In the distance I heard the sounds of snapping and crackling, mixed with the scurrying of terrified animals fleeing for their lives. It could only be what everyone in the piney woods dreads. Forest fire! And spreading fast, from the sound of it.

My heart cried out, *Oh, lordy, let me find P.D. before the flames spread to me!*

How could I find P.D. before the fire came any closer? How would the animals and birds survive? No rain had hit the piney woods since spring. The trees and undergrowth were dry as powder, and the flames were spreading quickly.

Now I was frantic to find some sign of P.D. The noise of animals rushing for safety, the chattering of birds high up in the trees swelled. Then I smelled the smoke, sensed the flames moving nearer. I had to go on. Oh, P.D., where are you?

The dogs had caught the scent of smoke, and their barking became frantic. The men were shouting. I heard Josh yelling at the top of his voice, "Annie! Get out of there! Get out quick!"

The smell of smoke filled my nose, and then I caught a glimpse of flames licking out from the underbrush. The whole world seemed to turn orange, yellow, and red right before my eyes.

I had never been so scared in all my life, and I spun around, ready to head toward the sound of Josh's voice. Suddenly, out of the burning woods came Vangie, walking like in a dream, pushing P.D. before her. But what a strange P.D. it was!

He stood there, finger in his mouth, clutching his bear, but looking like someone else's boy. He was in clothes I had never seen, an old-fashioned suit, much too small for him. His eyes pleaded with me, his face streaked with tears.

Vangie stretched out her hand, and for one wild moment I thought she would grab me and pull me into the the burning woods. Her mouth moved, but no words came out. Like snakes on fire, the flames leaped toward her, ready to grab her and P.D. too.

Suddenly, she pushed P.D. toward me, her eyes begging me to take him.

I didn't stop to think. I grabbed P.D. by the hand and yelled, "Come on, Vangie! Quick! Before the fire gets us. Hurry! Follow me! Josh is just ahead. He can get us out of here."

Keeping a tight hold on P.D., I beckoned her to follow me. She shook her head once, her hair, blending with the flames surrounding us, swirling about her head. And then, as I watched in horror, she gathered her tattered dress close around her and stepped back. As she stretched her arms out toward P.D., the searing flames engulfed her.

"No!" I screamed in horror, clutching P.D. to me. I was rooted to the spot, staring at the place where she had disappeared.

"Annie, move it!" It was Ben's voice, and I could hear the sound of feet running toward me.

"Annie, run as fast as you can!" Josh was close behind Ben, and I knew P.D. and I had to run for it.

Whooooosh! A tree limb, aflame and smoking, crashed to the ground in front of us, sending a shower of sparks in all directions.

With P.D.'s hand tight in my grip, I ran toward their voices. *Snap!* I felt a sharp pain in my leg, and I hit the ground. I was helpless, my foot caught by a fallen limb.

"Run quick, P.D.!" I yelled. "Run to Ben!" Smoke filled my nose and mouth, blinding my eyes. The scorching flames were so close I could feel the heat on my face and hands. I had never been so terrified in my life.

Then Ben was there, scooping up P.D. and running

like thunder out of the woods. I was alone! I couldn't move. Couldn't run. Fire surrounded me; smoke swirled everywhere. My whole world seemed to be engulfed in flames!

Then Josh's face loomed before me, and, with one massive heave, he shoved the limb aside. I felt him lift me up, the shelter of his arms holding me tight.

Limbs continued to crack and flames popped all around us. Fire was everywhere, licking and snarling at us as Josh sprinted for safety. I watched in horror as a tall pine, its limbs ablaze, crashed straight toward us. Then my whole world turned black.

CHAPTER 14
Good and Bad News

I woke to the sound of voices. My leg ached. My face felt raw and swollen. Worst of all, I smelled like a barbecue pit. But the most marvelous, most comforting thing in the whole world was Pa's face smiling down at me.

"So, you're back among the living?" Just having Pa near made me feel one hundred percent better.

I started to raise my head, but fell back on the pillow. Pa's face got serious. "Better take it easy for a while, Annie. Your leg's broken. I've set it in a temporary splint, but you've got burns on your face and hands."

"P.D.?" I croaked.

"Safe as houses," Pa assured me. "Thanks to my brave girl. Your ma's fit to be tied over you risking your life, though."

I groaned. Facing Millicent was not something I was wild to do.

"You took a mighty big chance there, Annie. But it was a chance that paid off. Your aunt and uncle can't wait to thank you themselves. And takin' chances is what life's all about." Pa gave me one of his smiles. "I guess my girl's growin' up."

Suddenly, I remembered. All the horror swarmed back into my mind. "Vangie? Did Josh get her out?"

Pa shook his head. "No, baby. Josh was busy rescuing you. Couldn't get to her in time. He and his pa found her body not too far from where Josh found you."

"It was Vangie who pushed P.D. out of the fire, Pa." I ached, knowing that she had died saving my little cousin. "I just shoved him toward Ben."

"Everyone did heroic jobs, darlin'. But you found P.D. Josh told us that you were the one who suspected he was with Vangie. We're as proud of you as can be. Callie can't stop singin' your praises, and Zeke's bustin' his buttons over your deeds today."

Then Pa's face grew serious. "But life is a strange mix of happiness and tragedy, darlin', and we've had even more tragedy."

"What?" I croaked, terrified that maybe Josh or Ben had been hurt.

"When Lige Carruthers and Josh got home, they found Zephyr dead, lying on her bed, holding an old snapshot of Vangie and her little boy."

"Oh, Pa." Hot tears swelled in my eyes. "You reckon she knew Vangie had died in the fire?"

"Zephyr'd been sick a long time, Annie. Bad heart. It was only a matter of time, and everyone knew it." Pa put his hand on my forehead. "But I've seen things in my lifetime that not even medical science could explain. So maybe she knew. Maybe she knew."

"What's gonna happen to Mr. Carruthers and Josh? How will they live?" I couldn't bear to think of Josh having to live all alone with only his pa.

"That's what your Uncle James H. and Zeke went over to talk about. Callie's gone to help with Zephyr's funeral, and Zeke made your ma and Aunt Dee go over to pay their respects." Pa smiled again.

"I bet they're havin' fits." I smiled up at Pa.

"Reckon so, darlin'. But right now I want you to get some rest. Time to talk later." Pa patted my swollen hand.

Questions swirled through my head, but I was so exhausted that I slept and didn't wake up until night. Callie was smoothing sheets, and she and Millie were talking in whispers. I kept my eyes shut, listening to what they had to say.

"Oh, Mama, just look at her. No eyebrows or lashes. Hair all singed. And a broken leg to boot. She'll be laid up 'til school starts." Millie was, as usual, all sighs and regrets where I was concerned.

"For garden seed, Millie. Hair will grow back. Limbs will heal. Annie's gonna be just fine. Right as rain by the time school starts. Try seein' beyond her looks for once. The girl's been through a terrible ordeal."

I heard Millie get up and swish from the room and Callie sigh in exasperation. Looks were all my mother thought or cared about. I opened my eyes, pretending I hadn't heard one word.

"Well, there you are. Awake at last." Callie began bustling about, sponging my face with cool water. "Your pa's lettin' me clean you up a bit, and your ma would like to see that hair a bit smoother, I'm sure. 'Fraid your curls are all gone." Callie didn't seem to miss those curls one bit, and neither did I.

"I stink so, Callie." I twisted around in the bed so she could wash my neck.

"Won't when I'm finished. I broke out a cake of Cashmere Bouquet for this sponge bath. Can't get to that leg, but at least you'll smell like a human again. There's a flock of folks rarin' to visit you. See how you're doin' and say their thanks."

When Callie had me halfway presentable, Uncle James H. and Aunt Dee came in with P.D. My aunt and uncle were all smiles, and P.D. snuggled beside me. He felt so warm and good, I couldn't help but give him a big hug.

"Wady took me to live in a tree. Gave me some

103

clothes, but they're too tight. We ate acorns for supper and drank creek water. You ever eat any acorns, Annie?" P.D. looked at me with a smile full of questions.

I could hardly believe my ears. Here was P.D., talking away! Words just gushing out of his mouth. P.D.—who could hardly manage two words a day!

Uncle James H. and Aunt Dee broke into laughter. "We wanted you to hear him yourself," Aunt Dee said. "We haven't been able to shut him up since his great adventure."

Uncle James H. came over to the bed and took my hand. "Your aunt and I are mighty beholden to you—and to Ben. You two saved P.D."

"It was Vangie who pushed him out of the flames," I replied. "And Ben who brought him out."

"And you who found him!" Uncle James H. patted my hand. "If it weren't for you, we'd be missing one boy tonight!"

Uncle James H. gave P.D. a big hug. "I knew there was some special reason that you were my very favorite niece," Uncle James H. continued.

"I'm your *only* niece," I replied with a smile.

"That's so," Uncle James H. said with a chuckle. "And I'm certainly glad to have you."

Ben brought me a supper tray, and Hadley and he waited while I finished every bite Callie had sent.

"I don't guess I'll ever understand what happened,

Ben," I told him, between bites of tapioca pudding. "I just couldn't get Vangie to come out. She could have made it, you know."

"I know." Ben's face was solemn. "Just seems like Vangie belonged to the woods."

We both were silent for a moment, lost in our thoughts.

"Oh, I almost forgot. There's someone else to see you, and I suppose you two want to be alone."

Ben grinned a wicked grin and took my tray. Hadley giggled just like the fool he was, and I knew it could only be Josh.

And there he was! Standing in the doorway, looking at me with those soft, brown eyes. Even with all the tragedy in his family, Josh had his special smile for me.

"Oh, Josh," I said, my heart going out to him. "I'm so sorry about your ma—and your sister. I really did try to get her to come with us."

"I know you did, Annie. Pa knows too. Vangie lived as she wanted, and, I guess, died as she wanted."

Josh sighed and sat down by my bed. "Ma's time had come, Annie. We all knew that."

"What's gonna happen to your pa now?" I asked, wondering deep inside what was going to happen to Josh.

"Mr. Zeke has talked him into going into the old folks' home in Woodville. That's where his brother is, so he'll have company. The two of them can play dominoes all day long and argue over who won."

Josh seemed to be pleased with this arrangement. "Mr. Zeke's gonna buy the house and the land, so part of the money will pay his room and board."

Zeke buying that old rundown shack? Well, I guessed my grandpa had money to burn, if he was buying that pig-in-a-poke.

Josh seemed to read my thoughts. "The land's worth somethin', and Mr. Zeke can sell Pa's bird dogs for a bundle," he said.

"But what'll you and Newt do for a home?" The thought of never seeing him again filled me with sadness.

"Ain't been home for some time, Annie. Ever since Ma turned sick." Sadness lay on Josh's face. "But I guess we'll not be needin' a home for a while. Newt's got three more years at Stephen F., and your pa and uncle think they can get me into the University of Texas. I've got the grades, you know."

My heart soared. "That would be wonderful."

"Yes," Josh went on, full of plans. "I want to study biology. Use what I know about the natural world and learn more. Your uncle's going to help with books and housing, and your pa's workin' on a scholarship. Helps that they are both grads. And Miz Callie and Mr. Zeke say Newt and I can come visit during vacations."

I hardly knew what to think. A million feelings zoomed through me. Relief that Josh would be near, and I would get to see him from time to time. But mostly thanks that my family was helping him get an education.

"I'm sorry about your leg, Annie. I did the best I could to get you out safe and sound." Josh was solemn again.

"You were my knight in shining armor. Rescuin' me just when I needed rescuin'." I smiled at him, as full of gratitude as I had ever been.

"Well, I'm gonna say 'so long' now, Annie. Your pa wants you to get your rest. But I'll be seein' you, and we'll have more swimmin' lessons."

With one last smile, the man of my dreams walked away, his mind, I knew, already at the university and his new life. I thought my heart would break, but it hardly had time to begin the breakin' process when Pa returned.

"Well, so Josh has told you his news." Pa sat down beside me.

"Yes, and it's mighty generous of you and Uncle James H."

"Nonsense. The boy's got the makin's of a fine biologist. All he needed was a little help. He'll make us all proud." Pa glanced toward the door.

"And you make me proud, Pa." We sat silently for a few minutes. He held my hand, and I was happy just being close to him and feeling safe again. The stars had come out, and I spotted my old friends, the fireflies, their tiny lights twinkling as bright as ever.

That night I dreamed about Vangie. Saw her again, her eyes so sad, her hands pushing P.D. toward me. Those arms stretching out toward him, as the fire consumed her.

Her hair, reaching out and then swirling into the flames, seemed to draw me toward her, and I woke in terror, covered with sweat. I lay there shivering, and I found that my cheeks were wet with tears. No matter how I tried to forget her, the memory of Vangie seemed to haunt me.

CHAPTER 15
Parties and Pianos

Well, here I was, laid up in bed again. My leg in a cast that made it itch worse than the chicken pox. Seemed like I'd spent half the summer staring at these bedroom walls.

I couldn't complain, though. Ozella had fixed all my favorite dishes. When Hadley whined that he wanted strawberry Jell-O with bananas, while I wanted lime with pears, she'd told him how "the cow ate the cabbage."

"Maybe someday, Mr. Wants-and-Needs, when you're a gen-u-wine hero, I'll fix you red Jell-O stuffed full of bananas seven days a week. Right now, if you want Jell-O, better gobble up the green." Ozella shook her apron at him while Mama's baby lapped up a big bowl of lime.

Uncle James H. put in a standing order at the bookstore near the hotel. Now instead of a Book-of-the-

Month, they delivered me a book every week. And Uncle James H. made the best choices.

I'd finished *Gone with the Wind* and was plowing through *Anthony Adverse.* Aunt Dee had sent a sappy teenage book, *Boys Are Like Streetcars,* which lay at the foot of my bed. I had read just one chapter and decided it would be a long wait before I got to Chapter Two.

Pa had decreed bed rest until my cast was off, and Millie came in each morning, delivering magazines and all the gossip in town. "Well, Anna, it seems you're quite the heroine. Everyone at bridge club was just full of questions about you." Then she was off in a whirl of rayon skirts.

Today, however, I'd skimmed all the magazines and read three chapters. I used to dream of days when I had nothing to do but read, but today I threw down my book in boredom. I hobbled to the kitchen to see what was going on, and found Ozella gossiping away with Josie, Hadley's old nurse.

"Lord, chile, just look at you!" Josie put down her glass of lemonade and peered at me over her spectacles. While Ozella was fat and jolly, Josie was as tall and lean as a string bean. Her gray hair had been treated and lay close to her head in glistening, marcelled waves. Today she was dressed in a bright red dress and felt hat I recognized as Millie's castoffs.

Josie prided herself on her style, and today Josie

was all style, her wrists jangling with gold bracelets. Josie's idea of style was often "the more, the merrier." And merry she did look and sound.

Now Josie was giving me the once over, and finding my style decidedly lacking. "That hair looks just like a haystack! And those eyebrows will never be grown back before your party!" Like her bracelets, Josie's words caught my attention.

"Party? What party?" I sat down at the table opposite her, all ears.

"There you go, Josie Baird, flapping those lips of yours!" Ozella brandished her rolling pin at Josie. "Miz Millie told you not to breathe a word about that party! Supposed to be a secret!" Shaking her head, Ozella turned back to the fried apple pies she was cutting out for supper.

"Come on, Josie. Tell all! I know you're just dying to!" I could wheedle anything out of Josie, who was as big a gossip as Millie.

Josie poured me a big glass of lemonade and leaned toward me. "Now, not a word to Miz Millie that I tole you. She'd skin me alive!"

"As well she should!" Ozella gave Josie a look of disgust.

"Your Aunt Dee's plannin' a big shindig for your birthday. End of August. Right on the twenty-sixth, just like always."

"I know when my birthday is, Josie. What about the party?" I was panicked. Maybe I could put a stop to Aunt Dee's plans. Wait until my hair grew out. Or at least until I had eyebrows again.

"It's not just the usual birthday," Josie continued. "It's a celebration of your heroic deed of snatching pore little ole P.D. from the fiery furnace."

"I know what happened, Josie. Remember, I was there." I could hardly wait to hear about the party.

"Sure you were, sugar. As sure as sunshine. The entire congregation of the Golden Rule African Methodist-Episcopal Church is just singin' your praises. Glory be to God!"

That bit of news really made me blush. Ozella and Josie were both members and often took me to their church. The singing and preaching sure beat that at St. Martin's Episcopal.

Josie took another swig of lemonade and helped herself to Ozella's gingersnaps, and I joined her.

"The party, Josie? The party?" I knew if Josie got onto what Ozella called "her Jesus bizness," she'd go zooming through the Old and New Testaments and my party would be lost somewhere between the gospels.

"Just you listen, sugar girl, because it's gonna be a gen-u-wine grownup affair." Josie took another bite of gingersnap. "Your Aunt Dee's invited fifteen girls and, saints be praised, sixteen boys! Just think of that!"

Josie dissolved into gales of laughter, and Ozella joined in, her body shaking with glee, pie crust flying to the floor.

Boys! I couldn't believe it! Aunt Dee could not have told Millie this! No way! Millie gave me little lunch parties for eight little girlfriends. All of us dressed up and miserable.

"Honey girl, she has hired Miz Nichols to prepare sixteen cake boxes, stuffed full of sandwiches, fruit, and no tellin' what all. There's gonna be a certain flower on top of each one. Each girl's gonna have a card with a flower on it, and the boys choose those picnic boxes, and match up the flowers to find a girl to share their picnic supper.

"Yes, ma'am. One gets Pansy; another, Rose. And one young gentleman's gonna claim Miz Annie Brooks, sure as Christmas comes once a year." Both Josie and Ozella sat smiling at me, waiting for my response.

"You sure Aunt Dee planned this?" I could hardly believe it. Aunt Dee's idea of a party was ice cream and cake around the country club pool with plenty of waiters to serve and clean up.

"Well, your Uncle James H. had his hand in the planning," Josie went on. "Your uncle is quite the party boy." Josie and Ozella dissolved into more laughter. "Yes, Mr. James H. is gonna lead the dancin' on the terrace under the twinklin' lights."

Josie waited for me to respond, but I just sat there with my mouth open, hardly believing what my ears were hearing. Dancing! Millie would have a fit!

"Yessiree, Mr. James H. has already picked out all the records. Went down to Warner's Juke Joint and got all the latest hits. Harry James! Tommy Dorsey! And wait 'til you hear—Mr. Xavier Cugat! Your uncle can't wait 'til you're out of that cast and ready to cut a rug."

Josie's toes were tapping and her fingers snapping. "He's gonna teach you to rhumba, and he's plannin' on leadin' a conga line all around that backyard," Josie continued. "Now ain't that somethin'?"

Somethin', it surely was, but I couldn't be sure what!

"Your Uncle James H.'s gonna be countin' on you to help him make the joint jump," Josie continued. "You better start puttin' on a party face and thinkin' about a new party dress."

Party dress! The very thought filled me with terror!

"Josie," I wailed. "What'll I do? I can't go to any party. You know what Millie'll stuff me into!"

I could tell by the look on Josie's face that she knew what I was thinking. Visions of pink organza ruffles, blue bows, and white patent-leather Mary Janes drifted through both our heads.

"Chile, you shore got a problem." Josie's brow furrowed with the worry of it all. "Bet Miz Millicent's out at those stores this very minute, choosing one of those childish doodads. No, sugar, you'll have to put your foot down!"

Josie fixed her eyes on me. "Now, Annie, you just tell your ma, you ain't gonna slip all those frou-frou flounces over your head no more. Make her know you gotta have some style. And your own style."

My chances of convincing Millicent I had any notion of what style was were as slim as Ozella becoming reed thin overnight and Josie a bleached blonde. Even slimmer!

"Honey girl, you shore got your work cut out for you. And a cross to bear, as well." Josie bowed her head, and I was afraid for a moment that she was going to start praying over me. Might as well, for it might be over my my dead body. That's what I'd be before I'd approach my mother about discussing style—mine or anyone else's.

"Well," Ozella interrupted. "Maybe I could slip in a word to your pa. Maybe right after he's eaten his second fried apple pie."

"Oh, Ozella, would you? I'll do anything in this world for you—anything. Pick up my room. Peel peaches all day long."

"We'll see." Ozella wiped her hands on her apron and smiled at me. I knew she would. Ozella never failed me, and my heart soared. Maybe there was a chance for this party after all.

"Now, Annie, you'll never guess. Ozella has another surprise for you. Has to do with the church." Josie was anxious to move on to another topic that did not involve Millicent.

"What surprise?" Ozella looked from Josie to me.

"You know, about Mr. Zeke and the church." Josie gave Ozella a glance.

Now I knew they were pulling my leg. In all my born days, I had never known Zeke to put his foot inside a church. Never heard him sing a hymn, although he told Bible stories to us, but always in his own folksy style.

"No, ma'am." Ozella pursed her lips. "You're the one tellin' tales out of school today. Might as well keep right on!"

Josie hardly missed a beat. "Well, you know that pianner we always wanted for the choir? Mr. Zeke donated it. Took out that big roll of bills he always keeps in his pants pocket and gave a one-hundred-dollar bill right to Sister Sukey and Sister Toinette. Their eyes nearly bugged out of their heads.

"Those girls went right out and bought that pianner Saturday, and had it delivered for Sunday service. Reverend Williams asked God to look with favor on Brother Zeke for his most generous gift. Now, what do you think of that?" Josie beamed at me, waiting for my reaction.

I hardly knew what to say. "It was a mighty nice gift," was all I could manage.

"Well, of course, it's only a used upright. But plays like the harps at the pearly gates." Josie raised her hands heavenward. "Sister Toinette can really make the rafters ring when she tinkles those ivories."

"A remarkable gift!" Ozella added, nodding her head.

"Of course, Annie, you're the inspire-a-tion behind that gift." Josie winked. "Mr. Zeke done told Sukey and Toinette he gave that pianner to the church 'cause his little grandson was saved from sure-as-certain death."

Zeke donating pianos! Aunt Dee giving parties!

While I was trying to absorb all these wonders, the sound of a car turning into the driveway set off alarms.

"Uh-oh!" Ozella whisked our glasses from the table.

"Better skeedaddle, both of you. Here comes Miz Millie with her arms loaded with packages."

"Lord, save us all!" Josie sprang for the side door, and I limped for my bed, pulling the covers over my head. It was definitely time for a long summer's nap. I dreaded thinking what horrors were nesting in Millicent's packages.

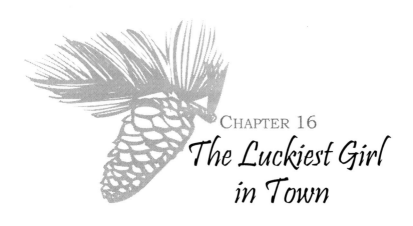

CHAPTER 16
The Luckiest Girl in Town

It was worse than even I could ever imagine! There stood Millicent at the foot of my bed, proudly displaying the most disgusting creation I had ever seen.

It was yellow, with tiny little pink flowers and a pink silk sash. I had expected puffed sleeves, but the ruffled hem was the end. This fashionable creation would be "okey dokey" for a kid of eight, but for a girl of fifteen it was a joke! I couldn't even bear to look at it.

I merely pulled the covers up over my head and groaned. Millicent was outraged and turned her wrath on me.

"Well, Miss, if that's all you can do, when Marjorie Rosenthal and I have spent the better part of a morning choosing you a birthday dress, I will leave you to your-self. I declare, you're just hopeless."

Hopeless I might be, but I would rather die than be stuffed into that horror. I remembered what Josie had said and stood my ground—if you can stand your ground with a broken leg.

I didn't catch even a glimpse of Millie all afternoon. I spent my time reading and thinking about Josh at college. Maybe I could go to Aunt Dee's party in shorts!

But Ozella had lived up to her word. When Pa came home, he brought Millicent into my bedroom. The dreaded party dress was nowhere in sight, but I just knew we were in for a knock-down-dragout.

"Well, Annie, your ma tells me that you don't care for the dress she chose for your birthday." Pa cast a quizzical glance at me.

I looked Millie right in the eye, hoping I could stare her into giving in. "No, Pa, it's too babyish. I'm going to be fifteen, not eight."

"I see." Pa looked from me to Millie, who did not look like she was going to give an inch.

"John, the dress is perfectly adorable. Do you want her going to a young people's party dressed like Theda Bara?"

Oh, Pa, I prayed. *Don't give in to her. Not this time!* I resolved I would stay home from my own birthday party rather than wear that awful dress.

"No, Millicent, I do not. But I think there should be a compromise between Theda Bara and Shirley Temple." Pa flashed me a wicked smile, proud of his wit. "Tell you what we'll do. Annie and I will save you a trip downtown. I've got to take that cast off her leg tomorrow anyway, so she can go to the office with me. I'll remove the cast, and we'll go over to the Bon Ton and see what else Mrs. Rosenthal has in stock." Pa smiled at Millie and then back at me.

"Very well, John." Millicent's voice was as chilly as the cold-storage vault at Zeke's plant. "I shall leave the choice of a birthday frock to you and Miss Priss here. I only hope that she is not the scandal of her aunt's lovely party."

Haughty as all get-out, Millie swept from the room, and Pa and I cheered silently.

"Well, Annie, we won that one. But don't think all of your battles with your ma will be that easy.

"Of course, you had some strong supporters. Ozella had her say over some mighty tasty fried apple pies, and I had a telephone call at my office from Miss Josie Baird on the subject of what, I think, she called your style. I didn't know you had any, but Josie assures me that it's developing. And Josie sure knows style if anyone does." Pa had that delicious twinkle in his eye that I loved.

"I don't know about style, Pa, but I know enough to know I've had enough of puffed sleeves and ruffles." I breathed a sigh of relief. Winning a battle with Millicent was exhausting.

Pa came through, as usual. The next morning, he

took off my cast and escorted me and the dreaded dress box to the Bon Ton.

"I think Annie would like something a bit more tailored, Mrs. Rosenthal." Pa flashed her a smile. "And a frock more suited to a young lady." Pa did have his winning ways with women.

"Of course, Dr. Brooks." Mrs. Rosenthal swept into the back room and reappeared almost instantly, her arms loaded with summer dresses.

She displayed them one after one, and Pa looked from each dress to me to Mrs. Rosenthal. My heart sank! Everything was either too fancy and fussy, or just too limp and drab.

Then, on the very last hanger, I saw it. I knew in an instant that I had found my style. I couldn't wait to try it on, smoothing the folds of its blue, green, and lavender plaid skirt, admiring the plain sleeves and collar, the tiny row of pearl buttons down the front. It wasn't Millicent's idea of a party dress, but it certainly was mine. And Pa agreed.

"Wrap it up, Mrs. Rosenthal. And Annie and I will look through your fall school clothes. Try to find some that suit her style."

Pa and I chose skirts, sweaters, blouses, and two plaid dresses that could go to Friday night football games. We left a beaming Mrs. Rosenthal and an extraordinary number of charges on our account.

Then Pa whisked me and our dress box over to my uncle's hotel for what he called "a bang-up lunch" in the dining room. Uncle James H. joined us, and all we talked about was the music for my birthday party. By the time Pa took me and my dress home, I felt like the luckiest girl in town.

•   •   •

I woke up early on the morning of my birthday. Pa came in to share his coffee with me while I ate breakfast on a tray. He brought in a small box, wrapped and tied with a bow, and I knew it was a special birthday present just from him.

Inside the box lay an antique cameo on a gold chain. "It was my mother's," Pa said, holding the cameo up for me to see. "You're so like her, I wanted you to have it."

"Oh, Pa." My eyes filled with tears. "It's the prettiest thing I've ever had." And it was! I gave him the biggest hug I could, holding him close, breathing in the spicy smell of his aftershave.

"Now, rest up, darlin', if you're going to jitterbug tonight. I don't want that leg giving out." He gave me a birthday kiss. "And I'll be home early to escort my girl to her party."

Later Millicent pranced in to give my hair a once over. Always in a hurry, she threatened to return that afternoon to set my hair in pin curls. "I suppose you'll have it all fly-away by eight tonight anyway."

I had barely settled back to my book when my door flew open and P.D. scampered in, clutching an object he thrust at me. It was a model of his hand cast in clay he had made for me in Vacation Bible School. On it the teacher had carved a date—July 30, 1947. Not my birthday, but the date of the fire. Not a date I was likely to forget.

"Happy birthday, Annie!" P.D. planted a big smack on my cheek, and just for a moment, the vision of Vangie, stepping back into the flames, flashed before me. What if she had pulled P.D. with her instead of pushing him toward me!

Then Callie and Aunt Dee brought me back to the here-and-now. They presented me with a box wrapped in silver and pink. I tore off the paper and looked in. There lay the most magnificent gift I had ever seen.

Wrapped in pink tissue lay a silver dresser set, mirror, comb, and brush. The comb was of silver and tortoise shell, and the mirror and brush were engraved with my initials. My fingers traced the letters—A and C with a huge B in the center.

"Just the thing for a high school girl." Callie beamed at me.

"It's beautiful," I breathed. "Oh, it's just gorgeous." The beauty of it just took my breath away. "Oh, thank you, Callie. Thank you, Aunt Dee."

"Your Uncle James H. has a special present for you, but he's using it tonight. A portable Victrola with enough records to dance your life away." Aunt Dee smiled her approval. "So, we'll see you tonight!"

"Not me!" Callie sighed. "Zeke and I are taking Ben and Hadley up to the camp. Get them out of your hair tonight. And Zeke wants to survey the damage to the woods. So, I'll just say 'Happy birthday' now, and many happy returns, sugar girl."

"I'll be there tonight, Annie, and I'm gonna dance. I think I'll just dance my life away too!" P.D. was proud as punch of himself.

"Yes, but Josie will be there to watch over him." Aunt Dee cast a glance at her son. I knew she was thinking what Callie and I were thinking—how close we had come to losing him.

I drew him to me. "You bet you'll dance, ole buddy. Maybe a wild tango under the stars."

"Sure," P.D. smiled and planted a big smack on my cheek. They were just leaving when Callie turned back.

"Oh, I almost forgot. Here's a letter for you. Addressed to you at my house. I suppose it might just be a birthday card." Callie's eyes held a wicked gleam. "Wonder who it's from?" she continued, knowing I could barely control myself. I wanted to snatch it from her hands and tear it open. "Well, I swan, it's stamped from Austin, Texas."

Finally, she handed it over, and I tucked it under my

pillow, not wanting her to know how badly I wanted to read it.

"Well, Dee, I guess we'll never know who that card is from. Gonna be a secret, I see. Guess we better be gettin' along, so somebody can read her mail."

Finally, they were gone. Fingers trembling, I drew out the card. It was covered with roses and the words "A Special Birthday Wish." Inside, in fancy script, it read "For a Special Person," but the real words Josh had written: "Hi Annie. College is gonna be great! Lots of labs! Hope you're fine. Newt and I will spend Thanksgiving with Pa. But I'll see you Christmas. Best, Josh."

My first love letter, and it didn't even have the word *love* in it. But it was from Josh to me, and that was all that mattered. And I'd see him at Christmas. It couldn't come soon enough!

I barely had time to tuck it back under my pillow to read again that night when my door opened again and Josie and Ozella came in.

"Mighty big doin's goin' on for somebody's birthday." Josie was all smiles. "Hear some young folks is gonna hidey-ho 'til midnight."

"And somebody I know is gonna have the best birthday cake in town," Ozella chimed in. "Coconut snowball."

"With lemon jelly fillin'—and enough to feed forty folks." Josie's eyes were wide with delight.

"A thousand thanks, Ozella."

"Well, here's somethin' to be even more thankful for." Josie put a package in my hands. "Small birthday token from Ozella and me."

The two beamed as I undid the twine and took out a small black Bible, stamped with a gold cross and my name in gold letters. The ends of the pages were all gold too.

"King James Version." Ozella was proud as punch, and I was too.

"To remind you that Jesus watches over his lambs, not just Mr. P.D., but Annie Brooks too," Josie added.

"Got a place for you to write in your husband's name and all your chilluns. Right inside." Ozella flipped the pages to show me where I could write in the names of a husband-to-come and at least ten kids.

"It's wonderful. Thanks to both of you." My heart was as full of happiness as it had ever been.

"Well, we'll see you later. I got a cake to frost. And Josie's got to get on over to your Aunt Dee's. Gonna help Pearlie May serve and ride herd on P.D.

"You and I will be travelin' together, you in the front seat of your pa's big ole Packard car. Me in the back, holdin' that birthday cake just so. Yes, ma'am, just like that 'gyptian queen floatin' on down that Nile River."

"Cleopatra!" I smiled at Ozella.

"That's the one, baby." Ozella beamed at me.

"Sure as God made little green apples. That ole Queen Cleo's gonna be me tonight."

CHAPTER 17
Lipstick and Somethin' Else

Aunt Dee's house was a beehive of activity. Everybody running around like chickens with their heads cut off, as Callie would say. High on his stepladder, Rufus swirled crepe paper around wires above the patio. In the kitchen Pearlie May poured fizzy ginger ale over chunks of lime sherbet.

Wild squeaks and honks came from the garden, where Uncle James H. was setting up the phonograph, while Josie tried to corral P.D. as he ran round and round the kitchen.

"Keep your fingers out of that cake frosting, Mr. P.D. Hampton, and yourself out of devilment, if you know what's good for you." Ozella shook her finger at P.D. "Lord knows you's a rascal—and a talkin' fool these days."

Giving P.D. a warning look, Ozella went to help

Pearlie May fill picnic boxes. "Better choose your flower, Annie. You want the prettiest, and you get first choice."

"I'll choose a camellia." I fingered the beautiful flower. "That's what I'd like to be."

"Put her name on it, Pearlie May. Annie's gonna be a camellia for tonight." Ozella went right on arranging daisies around her coconut snowball.

"Oh, and I'd better be careful how I put that matching camellia on this box. Be sure I get a good-lookin' fella to eat this picnic supper with Miss Annie Brooks." Pearlie May burst into peals of laughter, and Ozella joined in.

"Look at you, girl." Josie twirled me around and around. "That dress is something! Sure is! Your pa's sure done you proud. That dress has some style, or I don't know style when I see it!"

"Thanks, Josie! Pa let me pick it out myself."

"See, girl, I know'd you'd have style if you just had a chance to look it in the face. You can shore swing and sway with Mr. Sammy Kaye in that dress."

P.D. burst into a fit of giggles.

"Hush your mouth, sweet thang, or you don't get no cake—nor no chance to dance with me tonight." Josie gave P.D. a frown. "Now go on outside with your pop and let me add a few sparkles to Annie."

"I want some sparkles too!" P.D. clung to Josie's skirts.

"Sugar boy, your sparkles are all in your mouth since you started talkin'. Run along now . . . your time will come. *Shoo!*"

P.D. took off, and Josie ushered me into Aunt Dee's powder room, stopping to snip off a flower from a large arrangement.

"Let's see what this does." She fluffed my hair and tucked in the flower, securing it with bobby pins.

"That perks you up, honey. Sure does! Gives you a bit of color around your face." Josie stood back, pursing her lips and admiring her handiwork.

"This'll perk you up a whole bunch more!" With a grin, she drew a tube of Tangee from her apron pocket. "Went to the Kress store and got it for you myself! The perfect shade, if I might say so! Pink Passion!"

"Oh, Josie, Millicent's gonna have a conniption fit if I come out wearin' lipstick. You know she doesn't think I'm old enough." I looked with anguish at the tube of Tangee in her hand, longing just to taste it on my lips.

"Girl, your ma ain't studyin' you. She's out there with those other grown folks drinkin' Tom Collins and what all. She ain't gonna notice if you painted up like a clown, 'less you go out there and call attention to yourself, which I don't suggest you doin'."

Josie began screwing the Pink Passion toward the top, waving it in my direction. Squinting and sighing, she applied the color to my mouth until she was satisfied. Then she turned me toward the mirror, her face bursting into a wide grin.

"See what a difference a little color makes! Yes, ma'am!"

Even I could see the difference. My eyes seemed bluer! I looked not only fifteen, but maybe eighteen—at least.

"Just hope Millie doesn't catch sight of me!" I couldn't take my eyes off my reflection.

Josie stood behind me, her hands on my shoulders, smiling at me in the mirror, her red lips and "hotcha" earrings setting her own face aglow. "You the bee's knees, girl, the cat's pajamas!"

Then her smile turned serious. "Annie, look at yourself, hon. You no longer a chile. You a young lady. Your ma don't want you to grow up, 'cause that makes her seem older. And older is somethin' she's wantin' not to be."

Josie sighed again. "Right after I come to take care of Hadley, your ma told your pa she wasn't gettin' no older. She planned on stayin' twenty-five—for life. He could give her birthday presents—and the more elegant, the better—but it would always be for her twenty-fifth birthday. Just as if Millicent Brooks could make time stand still, just 'cause she wants it.

"Your ma plans always on bein' the Queen of the Southeast Texas Fair, or whatever she was back 'fore she married your pa. Tell the truth, if she had her way, she'd be Queen of the World."

I had to smile. That's exactly what Millie thought she was. And she encouraged Pa, Hadley, and me to think the same.

"Well, what Miz Millie wants and what she gets is two different things." Josie raised an eyebrow, and I caught her look in the mirror. "But that don't have nothin' to do with you. You are your own person! Ain't nothin' like her. Just ask your pa, if you don't believe me."

"Oh, but Josie, Millicent's so beautiful. Everybody tells her so!"

"Maybe she is; maybe she ain't. Not for me to say." Josie turned me around and gently shoved me down on the dressing-table stool. "But what I do have a say in is you, and I say you gonna be fine. Better'n fine."

"But I'll never be as beautiful as Millie," I sighed.

"No, you won't. Won't get no lies out of Josie's mouth. And I ain't gonna be Joan Crawford—or even Lana Turner. But I does all right." Josie grinned, as if remembering some particularly memorable Saturday-night conquest.

"But, like Ozella says, you got character, girl. And that counts for a whole heap in this world, just you wait and see. And now, thanks to Josie and your pa, you got some style. That'll take you a few places, to my way of thinkin'." Josie smiled, proud of herself.

"Once you get over tryin' to be Miz Millie, you gonna do fine. Lord, I remember when you was a little bitty thang and your ma and auntie took you to some fool ladies' 'do.' One of those high-toned ladies told your ma you'd never be as beautiful as she was.

"Now, your ma agreed and told that ole bossy fool that you'd just have to be 'somethin' else.' Well, your Aunt Dee almost had a hissy fit. Couldn't wait to get home to tell your pa."

Josie took time out to fluff my hair, pursing her lips to get it just right. I was all ears, wanting her to go on. "Well, you know your pa. He sees so much sufferin' in the world, don't much annoy him. He just rared back and let out a good ole belly laugh. 'Well, Dee,' he told her. 'Somethin' else is just what I had in mind for her.'"

Josie bent over laughing, and I joined in. "So, you see, baby, when anybody starts tellin' you what you ain't, you just look 'em in the eye and tell 'em what you is—somethin' else."

While I was pondering this bit of wisdom, Pearlie May let out a yelp from the kitchen. "Look what you done now, Rufus. You let that ole crepe paper mess fall in my punch. What's got into you, man? You gone plumb crazy? Them young folks don' wanna be drinkin' no crepe paper!"

"Punch's green . . . crepe paper's green. How you figure they gonna know the difference?" Rufus had few words to say, but he always liked to have the last one.

"Lord, I better get on out there! They gonna set up a ruckus, and your Aunt Dee'll have a fit." Josie smoothed her hair, checking out her own reflection in the mirror. "Now, get yourself together, girl. If my ears do not deceive me, I hear cars comin' up the drive. Bound to be your guests arrivin', and right on time!"

I threw my arms around Josie. "Thanks, Josie."

"Weren't nothin' but a tube of lipstick, girl." Josie flashed me a smile.

"Seems to me it was a whole bunch more." I smiled back at her.

"Well, just you remember it, sugar! You got style; you got lipstick. It's your birthday, baby, and you just go right on out there and shimmy and shine."

CHAPTER 18
Fifteen Candles

"Annie! Annie! Gosh, it's great to see you! I just love that dress. It's fabulous!"

"Gee, you missed a cool summer. Camp was great, and I made the canoe team!"

"I made the finals in tennis and had a part in the drama festival."

There was no doubt about it. Vallie Jean and Sissie had arrived, full of camp adventures, gushing as usual.

"It'll be better next year when you're with us. We want you in our cabin, and you'll love all the Cheyennes." Vallie Jean was already looking forward to next summer.

"Heard about you rescuin' your little cousin. Golly, Annie, everybody's talkin' about you!" Sissie looked at me, her eyes as round as the summer moon.

"Saw Miss Elkins in the drugstore," Vallie Jean

added. "She had even heard about your adventure and said you ought to write a story about it."

While I was thinking what I might write for our school paper, the boys arrived. Boys! Aunt Dee had won out! Boys were invited, and here they were, huddling in a little group, eyeing us like we were aliens who had zoomed down to Aunt Dee's garden in spaceships out of "Flash Gordon."

Some were predictable—Bob Robertson, son of Zeke's partner, and Sonny Graham, who lived next door to Callie and Zeke, and J.W. Watson, whose father owned the biggest hardware store in town.

But Aunt Dee had done her homework. She'd invited some junior-high school stars, the dreamboats of our class. Willy Walton, the tall, lanky, slow-talking captain of the basketball team, and Jackie Dickinson, short, wise-cracking, full of crazy jokes, the life of every party. The boys had gathered around Jackie, telling jokes and laughing, ignoring all of us completely.

Then Mary Martha Austin, prissy as all get-out in a green ruffled dress, sauntered over to the boys and, bold as brass, began talking a mile-a-minute and rolling her eyes at Willy. He just stood there like some goofus looking at her as if she'd gone plumb crazy.

But the boys got the message—better mix and mingle. Then a wild, Latin melody burst from the phonograph, and Uncle James H. and Aunt Dee were forming a conga line.

"One, two, three, kick! One, two, three, kick!"

With Uncle James H. leading the way, me second, and Aunt Dee shepherding the boys into line, like a lazy snake rising from its slumber, the conga line, with all of us shaking and kicking like Mexican jumping beans, lurched across the yard.

Whoops of laughter burst forth from the line, as Jackie's feet went every which way, and Willy stumbled to keep his long legs moving to the rhythm. Round and round the yard we went, Uncle James H. rolling his arms, Aunt Dee shaking her hips and tossing her head like Carmen Miranda.

Pa led the adults in applauding our efforts, and, wonder of wonders, Millicent joined in. When the music ended, we all burst into applause. Uncle James H. knew the true meaning of an ice-breaker. We wandered back to the patio to catch our breaths, but the talk and laughter never ceased.

It was time to choose partners for our picnic supper, and Pearlie May and Ozella handed each boy a picnic box and each girl a flower. Now it was up to the boys to find the partners by matching boxes to flowers.

Willy had trouble matching his flower, until Ozella, shaking her head and rolling her eyes, turned him in the direction of Carol Sue Ogden, as sweet and shy as the daisy she held. Neither would say a word all through supper.

Mary Martha was in a perfect snit because she was forced to share a picnic box with Arthur Wheeler, our class brain, a boy of myriad thoughts but few words. She threw down her rose in disgust and spent the whole suppertime making goo-goo eyes at Willy.

Vallie Jean, holding her pansy, grabbed Sonny and the picnic box and led him off to the arbor, while Jim Anderson found Sissie and her violet and joined them.

Then J.W. stood before me, smiling and holding our picnic box. "Well, Miss Camellia, I guess you're mine. At least for supper. I may not be Clark Gable, but I'm your gallant escort on this festive occasion."

J.W. made a mock bow before me. He prided himself on his wit, and I laughed and joined in. "Well, I'm not Claudette Colbert, but I will be your Miss Camellia. At least for supper."

We all tore into the picnic boxes, and the sandwiches and fruit disappeared like wildfire. Then Pearlie May and Ozella circulated with two trays heaped with more sandwiches. Willy helped himself to two handfuls until Ozella slapped one hand, and he meekly returned two to the tray. But there was plenty for all.

Now it was time for the cake, and *oohs* and *aahs* resounded as Ozella carried it in, fifteen candles flickering. Everyone gathered round, shouting, "Make a wish,

Annie! . . . Tell us what it is! . . . What you gonna wish for, Annie?"

The night sky had darkened, and a million stars spilling down the Texas sky shone brighter than the fifteen candles on my birthday cake. As I looked out at Uncle James H.'s smiling face, I wondered about the changes that had taken place in my life in just one summer. What was there about the fairytale magic of a birthday that made you feel that life had really moved on? Did those fifteen candles on Ozella's coconut snowball cake spell the end of my childhood? Had I, as Josie predicted, really become a young lady?

I sighed, looked up at my friends with a smile, and blew out the candles. I was telling no one what my wish was! Ozella began cutting slices, and Josie passed around plates. Pearlie May served up the punch, and the only sounds were slurps and giggles. The boys gulped down cake, washing it down with punch, and the girls took dainty bites.

Finishing my own slice, I headed out to the yard, just to savor the moment, to impress on my memory forever the happiness of this birthday night.

Uncle James H. was putting on more records, signaling that it was time to dance, and the strains of Artie Shaw's "Begin the Beguine" floated up from the garden. I stood for just a moment, listening to the haunting melody that reminded me of all the exotic people and romantic places I longed to see.

Josie and P.D. were caught up in the rhythm, swinging and swaying in the moonlit garden. Josie sashayed her hips to the music, while P.D., laughing as he twirled, reached his hands toward the stars, just as he had once reached for "flybutters."

I stood still, savoring the scene. Then my mind wandered back to the piney woods that had caused me such pain and heartache. The woods now blackened and burned, but that Zeke told me would soon grow back. I wondered if those woods would ever hold such wonder and mystery for me again.

Next year I would be off to summer camp, and the next year too. Then I'd be off to college. Perhaps the woods of my childhood would never be the same again. Still they would be there, clinging to their age-old mysteries, holding their wonders for others to discover.

One thing I was sure of, though. Village Creek would always be there, timeless as ever, twisting and turning, moving ever onward, mysterious and deep. It had seen our sorrows and the sorrows of others, and still it moved on, holding our secrets within its depths.

Vangie had been part of those woods, part of the wonder and mystery of the creek. She had been born of the woods and water, and perhaps she had returned to them. But I knew, no matter what life would bring for me, Vangie would always live in my memory.

Suddenly, an odd feeling came over me, a haunting, shivery feeling, and I knew Vangie was near. At first I sensed her presence, then saw her image, only a faint glimmer at first, swirling out of the limbs of Uncle James H.'s oak trees. The same wild, twisted red hair framing her face, her eyes glowing deep emerald, but her lips caught in a faint smile.

This image of Vangie no longer held fear and terror for me. No longer was she the wild spectre, "The Ghost of the Pines." She seemed happier, no longer grief-stricken, more at peace.

Her eyes gazed longingly, but happily, at the wildly cavorting P.D. Her smile hung like a low-lying moon for a mere moment among the leaves, and then her image began to fade slowly into the night, strands of her hair melting in the darkness like pools of strawberry ice cream.

It seemed that the stars reached down to claim her, the moon to hold her for one endless second in its orbit. And then she was gone. I raised my hand in farewell, thinking perhaps I had only imagined her, conjured her up from my memory of the woods and water I loved.

And then I saw P.D., standing still as a ghost in the moonlight, his hand reaching out toward the heavens. Wherever Vangie was, wherever she had gone, P.D. had sensed her presence too. All too briefly, my little cousin had embraced his "wady," perhaps only in his imagination, maybe only as a soon-to-be-forgotten dream.

Then the spell was broken. Laughing to the music, moving to her own rhythm, Josie caught P.D. up and turned toward the house. P.D. blew me a kiss and shouted, "Happy birthday, Annie!"

"And many more!" Josie echoed.

As if sensing my mood, Uncle James H. changed the record. The strains of "Moonlight Serenade" flooded the night. Who could resist that melody, my favorite of that summer? Who could keep their feet from tapping when Glenn Miller's trombone slid down the summer night?

No one, it seemed. Everyone was choosing partners. Uncle James H. caught Aunt Dee in a tight hold, dipping and swaying to his own magical rhythm. Pa held Millicent close, smiling down at her, her pale chiffon skirts swinging to the music. Mary Martha pulled Willy out to the yard, clasping him close and looking up dreamily into his eyes. Vallie Jean was locked in Sonny's embrace. Sissie had even coaxed Bob to dance to that lilting melody.

As the music swelled, J.W. stood before me, his arms held out. "How about a dance, birthday girl?"

Smiling behind the thick lenses of his glasses, his eyes met mine. Perspiration beaded his forehead, and his hand felt hot and sticky as he took mine.

The music surrounded us, and soon J.W.'s arm was pumping away, his feet moving in a perpetual box step, his sweaty hand clutching the back of my dress. What did I care! I was fifteen. Music was playing, and I was dancing!

As if drawn by the music, hundreds of fireflies swarmed out of the summer night, swooping down among us, their twinkling lights mingling with the glow of the Chinese lanterns and the stars.

Over J.W.'s shoulder, I watched them, fascinated. Perhaps they were the same fireflies that had witnessed my piney woods adventure, the ones that had given me hope when there seemed none. Oh, if only their glimmer and glow would light all my nights and brighten all my lazy summer evenings!

For one magical moment, there with the music surrounding me, smelling the sweet perfume of the flowers from my Aunt Dee's garden, there with the night sky enfolding me, I imagined that those twinkling fireflies, like my family and friends, would be mine forever.